# Beautiful Blue World

## ALSO BY SUZANNE LaFLEUR

*Eight Keys*

*Listening for Lucca*

*Love, Aubrey*

# Beautiful Blue World

## SUZANNE LaFLEUR

WENDY
LAMB
BOOKS

Wendy Lamb Books and the colophon are trademarks of
Penguin Random House LLC.

Visit us on the Web! randomhousekids.com

Educators and librarians, for a variety of teaching tools,
visit us at RHTeachersLibrarians.com

*Library of Congress Cataloging-in-Publication Data*
Names: LaFleur, Suzanne M., author.
Title: Beautiful blue world / Suzanne LaFleur.
Description: First Edition. | New York : Wendy Lamb Books, [2016] | Summary:
Sofarende is at war and the army is paying families well to recruit children, so if
twelve-year-old Mathilde or her best friend Megs is chosen, they hope to help their
families but fear they will be separated forever. | Description based on print version
record and CIP data provided by publisher; resource not viewed.
Identifiers: LCCN 2016021125 (print) | LCCN 2015046201 (ebook) |
ISBN 978-0-307-98033-5 (eBook) | ISBN 978-0-385-74300-6 (hardback) |
ISBN 978-0-375-99089-2 (lib. bdg.) | ISBN 978-0-307-98032-8 (pbk.)
Subjects: | CYAC: War—Fiction. | Survival—Fiction. | Best friends—Fiction. |
BISAC: JUVENILE FICTION / General. | JUVENILE FICTION / Family /
General (see also headings under Social Issues).
Classification: LCC PZ7.L1422 (print) | LCC PZ7.L1422 Be 2016 (ebook) |
DDC [E]—dc23

The text of this book is set in 12-point Caslon.
Interior design by Heather Kelly

Printed in the United States of America
10 9 8 7 6 5 4 3 2 1
First Edition

*For Amy*

with gratitude for days spent at
Bletchley Park and Dover Castle
and on countless other adventures

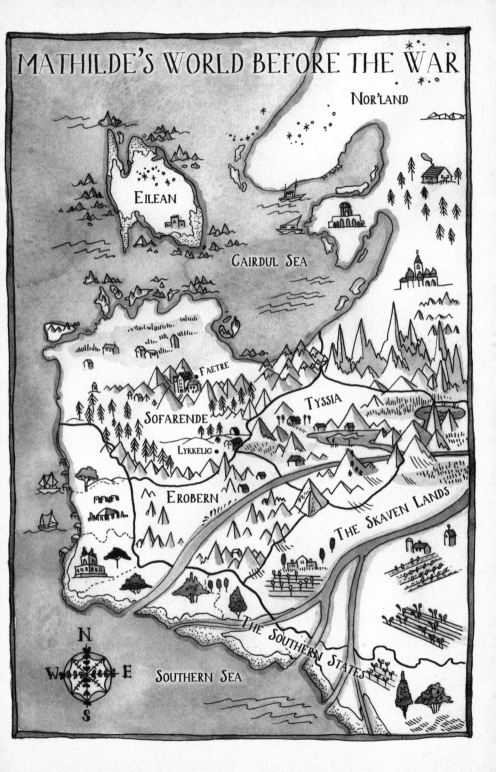

## CITIZENS OF SOFARENDE:

Due to the continued conflict with Tyssia, please be advised of new mandatory safety instructions.

Be on alert at all times for the sirens.

At the sound of the sirens, proceed immediately to your assigned shelter. Do not leave your shelter for any reason. Remain there until the all-clear siren sounds.

Shelter assignment:

Residence: Joss, 52 Raken Street, Lykkelig

Shelter: Heller, basement level, 54 Raken Street, Lykkelig

# 1

MEGS AND I FROZE on my front step.

We'd seen the notices on our walk home, pinned to every door, fluttering in the chill winter breeze: white butterflies tacked down, wishing to fly free.

It was better to think of them that way, like butterflies.

Because they also looked like white flags of surrender.

"Did you get one?" I asked, craning my neck to check two doors down, where Megs lived.

"Everyone did."

I looked at her, my best friend and opposite-twin, her dark braids mirroring my light ones. She realized the edge in her tone. It had snuck in, at least once a day, since her father had left to fight. Been ordered to fight.

*It's not you she's mad at.*

Her bright blue eyes, watering in the cold, took me in. A smile came to them as one appeared across her pink, chapped cheeks. "Come on, let's see what mine says." She offered her hand, led me past the Hellers' between us, to her own house. "See, we're assigned together! Whatever it is, it won't be so bad, Mathilde."

"But—why do we need shelter assignments?"

Mother, waiting for me to get home, opened our front door. She saw me and smiled, lifted her hand to wave. But then she spotted the notices across the street and turned to read ours. She grew very still; her smile disappeared.

Mrs. Heller opened her door, too. She read her notice, looked around at all of us. Her face swelled like a boiled red potato.

"Now you're going to be living at my house?"

"Living? How long do you expect us to be down there?" Mother asked.

"Who knows? Maybe forever. But your family's not to become a burden on our family; you'd better send over some food stores—"

"Food stores? I'm not sending my food stores over to your basement. You'll eat them!"

"Are you accusing me of being a thief?"

"That's what you've implied I am!"

My little sisters came to the doorway: Kammi, who had beaten me home from school, and Tye, blouse untucked and short braids falling out. I raced home, Megs at my heels. "Come on," I said to my sisters. "Come inside."

I quickly shut the door. The house was cold. There wasn't enough fuel for fires during the day anymore.

"Here, Tye, let's find your sweater." A sweater that had once been mine, and then Kammi's, and now had patches on the elbows.

"Catch me!" Tye shrieked.

She didn't need to know that I felt wobbly, that we might be headed to live in the basement next door. I chased her into the living room, grabbed her by the ankles, and held her upside down.

"I'm upside down! I'm upside down!" She giggled.

Poor Tye had never known the world right-side up. Before Tyssia decided they wanted all of it for themselves; before they took over the Skaven lands, before they joined with Erobern.

Before they were coming for us.

Mother came in and slammed the door. I dropped Tye, who rolled away, laughing.

"Why are we going to the Hellers' basement?" I asked Mother.

"Ours is too shallow."

"Too shallow for what?"

I followed her into the kitchen, where she loaded up a box with tins and jars. There hadn't been that much in the pantry to begin with. *Don't grumble, don't grumble,* I told my stomach as the shelves emptied.

Mother handed me the heavy box, adjusting the red scarf around my neck and freeing my braids. "Take this next door."

Was she afraid, like Mrs. Heller, that we were going to have to *live* in their basement?

For how long?

Forever?

I looked at Megs, who shrugged.

"Why don't you do your homework at Megs's house?" Mother said.

"Why is she mad at you? You didn't ask the government to send those notices."

And wouldn't Mrs. Heller want to help us, if there was some kind of emergency? She was our neighbor. Kammi played with her daughter.

Mother smiled, grazed her knuckle down my cheek. "Don't you worry. Run along."

Megs and I walked to the Hellers' in silence. Megs knocked. When Mrs. Heller answered, she looked less like a boiled potato, but she took our box with a huff and slammed the door.

"It's probably like a drill," Megs said as we walked to her house. "Like fire drills at school. We practice those all the time, and have we ever had a fire? No. We'll probably never have to go to her stupid basement."

She ripped down her family's notice on the way through the door. She stopped to look me in the eye.

"Even if we do, we'll be together. Whatever happens, I'll be with you."

# 2

I DREAMED OF SUMMER.

Sun bright, woods green; Megs smiling and sparkling, skipping along with her hand in mine. The way we spent all the best days, headed to the stream, shoes and socks forgotten.

The war forgotten.

But Megs pulled away from me suddenly and started wailing.

"Megs?"

She didn't seem to hear me. She kept screaming.

"Megs!"

I couldn't shout loud enough for her to hear me; the sounds caught in my throat.

Then it was dark.

I wasn't in the woods anymore.

I was in my room.

It wasn't Megs wailing.

Sirens!

I hauled my sisters out of their bed.

Kammi hurried down the stairs in front of me; Tye, only five, remained limp and drowsy and confused. I scooped her up, her head drooping on my shoulder as I rushed downstairs.

We found our coats and shoes at the front door, hung on hooks and lined neatly in a row, the way we always left them.

Father hurried down the stairs, straightening his green street-patrol uniform.

"Why are you wearing that?" I asked, shouting over the sirens. "It's not your night."

"Everyone from Street Safety has to report if the sirens go off."

He met my eyes in the dark.

If he didn't go, he could be fined. Or imprisoned. Or worse—taken to the border to fight. Even though he was older than most soldiers. Even though he was our father and we needed him.

Mother appeared behind Father, her face tight as she looked away from him to her girls, counting us in one glance. She met my eyes, too, but only for a second.

We were to go to the Hellers' basement to await the catastrophe.

Father was not.


"Be good, Big." Father brushed his nose lightly against my ear.

I used to be Little, a long time ago, before Kammi came, but since she was born when I was four, I have been Big. When Tye came, Kammi became Middle. Little, Middle, Big.

He added, "You're *all* my Littles. Always."

Then he was gone, out the front door.

Up and down the street, people raced across footpaths and yards.

Megs's mother, Mrs. Swiller, ran toward us, a baby and a toddler on her hips, two more little children running with clasped hands behind her, struggling to keep up.

"Where's Megs?" I stopped.

Mother lifted Tye from my arms. "Let's go, Mathilde."

"She'll be right behind us." Megs's mother said it like she expected it, not like she had checked.

But I would. I wouldn't go down into the cellar without Megs.

Especially not if we were going to have to live there *forever.*

Aerial engines roared above us.

"Mathilde!" Mother yelled from the basement doorway.

The engines roared louder and I looked up as aerials appeared in the searchlights.

Great winged, flying machines of metal. Built for war.

Orange and black striped their wings.

Black for Tyssia, orange for their recent union with Erobern.

Our enemies.

*Come on, Megs.*

"Mathilde!" Mother yelled again.

*Come on, Megs! You promised you would be here with me.*

I counted the aerials, the moments. . . .

*One, two, three . . . seven, eight . . .*

Where was she?

Why wasn't her mother waiting, calling her like my mother was calling me?

It would kill me if Megs didn't make it, but another glance at Mother told me that *she* was going to die, right now, this instant, if I didn't get under cover.

So I ran to catch up with Mother, my heart seeming to tear.

But before I reached the door, a hand was in mine. A dark braid swung into view as someone hurtled ahead to drag us into the basement.

Megs had made it.

A single candle stub burned in the center of the bare cement floor.

"But that's it," Mrs. Heller announced. "You should have brought your own candles."

The three Heller children lay on a mattress on the floor, cozy and sleepy, not having had to run outside to get here, still feeling safe in their own home, even if it was the basement.

Our mothers hadn't gotten us mattresses. Maybe they hoped it wouldn't be long. Maybe the aerials would just fly overhead quickly and we'd be back home in a few minutes.

Like a fire drill, like Megs had said. No real fire.

Megs's brothers and sisters huddled in a nervous heap around their mother, squishing like the sleeping family of kittens Megs and I had discovered in a hollow tree in the woods. Mother had Tye in her lap, having eased her into her coat, and Kammi sat next to them, her hand in Mother's, though she sat up straight, wide awake.

I let go of Megs for a minute and went over to Mother. I squeezed her other hand. "I'm sorry."

Her breath seemed too fast, too shallow. She gave me a thin smile. Not quite ready to forgive. But she loved me. So much it could drive her crazy. It was plain as the cement floor. But also as something prettier.

The sky. It was plain as the sky. A crystal-blue sky.

I leaned in to kiss her cheek.

"We're all here now," she whispered. "You can go sit with Megs."

I nodded.

But we weren't all here. Father wasn't. I knew she felt that, too, though she wouldn't let herself say it.

There were no fathers with us. Mr. Heller, like Megs's father, was a few years younger than mine and had also been sent to fight. Nobody who'd been sent to fight had come back. I'd been relieved Father was too old, but what was the difference? He'd been separated from us anyway, and we might never see him again.

I joined Megs sitting against an empty stretch of wall.

"What took you so long?" I asked.

She shrugged.

We told each other everything; why couldn't she answer me?

"This isn't so bad," Megs said. "If there was more light, we could study or read or draw or something. It could be like a sleepover."

She meant to help me feel better. But pretending it was a sleepover wouldn't make me forget that Father was out there, somewhere. In danger. I didn't dare explain with Mother and Kammi listening. I didn't want them to worry even more.

The rumblings of aerial engines increased, as if dozens flew over all at once. Then came thuds and pops. With each burst, the house rumbled above us.

I looked up at the ceiling. Mother let out a long, strained sigh.

Was this basement too shallow, too?

The thudding, popping bursts grew closer together. Louder. Overlapping.

The pops shook the ground. We jumped.

Depending on who jumped first, Megs and I would give the other's hand a squeeze. Twice we squeezed too early, waiting for the jump when no pop came. We both giggled.

Probably not the best time to do that.

Mrs. Heller erupted. "Fighting right over our heads now, aiming to kill us all."

Mother shushed her. "You'll frighten the children."

"I'm getting mine out of here, quick as I can." She nodded toward her children. "You'd best do the same. Sign your oldests up for that test. Maybe that's the way out."

My eyes met Mother's.

The posters had appeared a few weeks ago:

CHILDREN AGES 12–14

SERVE YOUR COUNTRY NOW!

SIGN UP FOR THE ADOLESCENT ARMY

APTITUDE TEST AT YOUR SCHOOL!

We were children age twelve, me and Megs.

We hadn't spoken of it. Not me and Mother, not me and Megs.

What did the army want children for?

Mother held my gaze, then said to Mrs. Heller, "Do we know it's better?"

"They could be teaching them to fly aerials. The lighter the bodies, the better. But maybe they're just going to keep them safe, deep underground, so when our whole world is gone, there will be someone to remember it. Make those smarties memorize all of history."

The whole world, gone?

"Anything would be better than sitting here," Mrs. Heller said.

Mother was still looking at me.

The candle puffed out suddenly, and I was glad.

But Megs's grip on my hand had become a little looser.

The second round of sirens—the all-clear—sounded about two hours before dawn, and we trudged home to our beds. The air outside had a thick, sour smell, the sky an orange glow.

The aerials were gone.

They had been replaced with shouts, and wailing; not mechanical sirens, but human ones.

Mother hurried us inside. She didn't even let us pause to hang up our coats.

"Can Father come home now?" Kammi asked.

"Go to bed; he should be here soon." But a new crease across Mother's forehead said that she had no idea when, or whether, to expect him. Normally he'd be home by seven a.m. But with that strange glow in the sky . . . that smoke . . . the shouts and cries . . .

Tye was still sleeping as I lay her in her bed.

"Can I get in with you instead?" Kammi whispered.

"Course."

We climbed into my bed with our coats on. The room was cold, and my sheets felt crisp as I covered us.

"Will we see Father again?" Kammi whispered. I knew she didn't want Mother to hear.

"I think so."

"Was that . . . bombing?"

"I think so."

"Other places have been bombed. I've seen them in news pictures."

"That's true." My mind had always struggled to understand the black-and-white newsprint photos; it looked like they showed the empty shells of buildings.

"But here was always safe. We were always safe. Father was always safe."

"Shh . . . shh . . ." I ran my fingers down her face, smoothing her hair back, wiping hot tears off her cold cheeks. "It's okay now. It's okay. You can sleep."

But I didn't sleep until her breathing slowed and I was sure that she had gone first.

# 3

MY EYES FELT GLUED TOGETHER, but I didn't try to go back to sleep.

No, something had woken me.

The kitchen was warm and smelled of coffee and milk.

My arms wrapped around him, my face pressed against his.

"Father!"

He laughed, setting down his steaming mug to hug me. "How'd it go, Big?"

"Fine. How did—" But I caught sight of Mother's face and sat down at the table for my tea and toast.

Kammi appeared in the doorway and flung herself at Father like I had, but she stayed in his lap, even though she was eight years old, and Mother, smiling, brought over Kammi's plate and mug and set them at Father's place.

Tye showed up last and asked, "Why am I sleeping in my coat?"

And, despite everything, the rest of us laughed.

• • •

But as we got ready to head out the door to school, Father drew me aside. "Take Kammi down Heldig Street; don't go any farther east than that."

"Why?"

"Some of the streets that way got hit. I don't want her to see it. Just head west, not east."

"Okay."

"Promise now?"

I nodded.

Dust—or ashes?—lined Father's clothes. His eyes looked puffy and tired.

How *had* his night been? What had he seen? What had he done?

I pressed into him in a tight hug, first getting a whiff of that odor from the bombing, then searching out the smell I knew. The post office, where he worked during the day—paper and sealing glue and cedar sorting boxes. I found it, breathed in deeply, and relaxed.

"Be good, Big. Don't forget which way to go."

"I won't."


Kammi's wooden soles slapped the frozen gray cobblestones as she hurried up the street ahead of me, though she turned around to look back every minute or so. Her bare knees between her skirt and kneesocks grew red and then white in the cold; her braids swung loose from her scarf.

I was curious about what had happened east of Heldig Street, but I wouldn't break my promise to Father.

Though he'd only said not to take Kammi there. He hadn't said anything about not going there on my own later.

"Mathilde!" Megs caught up with me. "I was worried that they'd cancel school."

"Mother and Father seemed to think we were still having it."

"I hope we are. I hope the school wasn't hit."

We continued up the street in silence for a few more minutes, past a closed bakery and one that was still open, though the window was half empty; past a cobbler who had doubled the size of the sign that said REPAIRS; past a butcher: MEAT TODAY—WHILE IT LASTS!; past the bookshop that hadn't been repainted in years, the books themselves crumbling and yellow.

A lot of people were out, but they didn't look like they were on their way to work. Some wore blankets around their shoulders instead of coats. They leaned against houses or on steps, holding steaming tin mugs. They all looked lost. Was it—was that man's hair singed off?

There were children, too. Why didn't I recognize them? They were from my neighborhood. But their eyes were big and scared, their faces smudged with gray dirt.

Kammi, several yards ahead, skipped along, not noticing these things.

We passed a poster: TAKE THE ADOLESCENT ARMY APTITUDE TEST!

"Megs?"

"Mm?"

"What do you think they'll have the children do?"

"They'll probably find them places to stay."

"No, not these children. The ones who take the test."

"Oh. On the test? Or . . . after?"

"After."

"I don't know."

Aerials buzzed low overhead. We looked up to see our own blue-green crest markings on them.

A whole fleet of aerials, heading east.

To our borders.

Or perhaps beyond them. Into the expanding lands of Tyssia. We had been at war for a year already, though our borders had held. But with Tyssia joined with Erobern, we had to defend thousands more miles. Soon the only safe place in Sofarende would be up north, along the Cairdul Sea. Tyssia and Erobern didn't have access to the sea.

We walked in silence for a few more minutes, and then she said, "They wouldn't send children to the front lines. They wouldn't."

Nobody would bomb children in their beds, either.

At least, I used to think nobody would.

Megs kept her eyes straight ahead, her mouth set tight.

An *I love you* for her caught in my throat. To say sorry. That I hadn't meant anything.

That I just didn't want anything to happen to her.

She turned and squeezed my hand, looking much more like her normal self.

"Don't," she said before I could speak. "I already know."

# 4

MY CLASSMATE KARL had gotten out of his house before it was bombed to bits.

But his uncle hadn't.

Now Karl didn't have a house.

Or an uncle.

Miss Tameron couldn't even tell us that he had stayed home, as he had no home to stay in. She just said, "Karl will not be in attendance today. It's my hope that he will be with us tomorrow. I'm relieved that all of you are here. I'm glad to see each of you."

An emotional statement. People were either not sharing such thoughts or spreading rumors. Our teacher had entertained the idea that some of us might not make it through the night. A frightening thing for any adult to suggest.

But Miss Tameron smiled, and her gladness filled me, too. Saying she'd been afraid for us also meant she cared what became of us. That we each still mattered, separately. Not just our country. Us.

We settled in to comparing ancient poems from Eilean

and Nor'land, our neighbors to the north, across the sea. As always, Megs answered all of Miss Tameron's questions.

I didn't answer any.

My eyes kept fixing on Karl's empty chair.

At the end of the school day, Miss Tameron handed everyone a form.

"Many of you have had your twelfth birthdays, so I'm obligated to give you these. Take them home and discuss this opportunity with your parents."

Across the top of the paper was the same call to service as on the posters, with the date the test would take place at our school, three weeks from now.

But the form made promises that the poster had not: that your family would receive four hundred orins—the highest unit of our currency—plus twenty a week more while you served.

You would be provided with room and board for the duration of your service and, at eighteen, your university education.

Room and board—that meant you would no longer be at home.

Across the bottom were lines for name, date of birth, and permission from both parents. And the sentence "I understand that applying to sit the test commits me to service should I be selected."

I scrunched up the paper and crammed it into my book bag.

I would show it to Mother and Father because I had been asked to, but I didn't want to sign up. I wouldn't go away from home.

Several of the boys were excited; on the way out, they mentioned flying aerials and boot camp and seeing some action and finally getting to take part. They'd been wishing the minimum age for the army was lower. They were tired of their fathers and older brothers being away while they could do nothing to fight the shortages or defend Sofarende.

Megs remained in her seat, studying the form. When she noticed me waiting, she folded it carefully, and put it inside her bag.

Megs, Kammi, Eliza Heller, and I left school together. We got to the end of the first block, and I started to slow.

"What is it?" Megs asked.

I shook my head at her and spoke to my sister instead. "Kammi, go home this way. Go straight there, okay?"

Kammi would be happy and safe with Eliza. It wasn't unusual for them to walk together. The two grabbed hands and started toward home.

Megs studied me as I watched them go.

"I want to see what happened," I said. "During the night, I mean."

"*Should* we go over there, though?"

"Were you told not to?"

"No."

"Me neither. Just not to take Kammi."

Megs bit her lip, considering.

"I just want to know. I just want to know what we're hiding from."

She nodded. We headed east.

• • •

In the still-rising dust and smoke, our shoes crunched on the cobbles. Overnight, they'd been covered in gravel.

Megs reached for my hand, and I took hers, glad for the warmth of her fingers.

There was no sign of what had been two rows of houses.

Of homes.

Of families.

Just heaps and heaps of rubble, as if someone had knocked down a mountain.

Only a few blocks from where we lived. It could have been our street.

Maybe it would be, tonight.

We continued up the center of the street as if on a strange conveyor, afraid to stop, afraid to hurry.

Spots of orange emerged in the gray: helmets and vests of rescue workers. They shouted to each other.

They were still finding people.

Still moving rocks and charred timber to open pathways to the basements.

But they were also carrying stretchers covered with sheets.

A row of these stretchers lay on the ground.

A woman ran up to the men in orange vests.

"Have you seen my son? My son? My son and his children, they live on this street!"

Lived.

There was no more street.

Nobody lived here anymore.

The woman ran on to the next set of rescue workers.

"My son! My son!"

Her words stabbed me behind my breastbone. My eyes followed her frantic path up the street.

"Mathilde?"

Megs was tugging my arm.

"Mathilde, we should go home."

I hung up my coat and scarf, tossed my shoes into the row by the door, and thundered upstairs.

I opened my math textbook and answer booklet on the small desk in our room. I sharpened my pencil, found my extra eraser, and wrote the assignment heading.

And then I just sat there, tapping the pencil.

I closed my eyes.

I could hear Mother's voice, pleading with the rescue workers: *My husband, have you seen him, he's on Street Safety Patrol? My husband!*

I wrapped my arms around myself as if to shut out her imaginary screaming; I rocked back and forth. Sweat beaded on my upper lip.

The voice changed to be Father's as he climbed through rubble in an oddly orange, smoky dawn: *My wife, my daughters! We lived here, on this street!*

"Big!"

The shock of the strength of his voice jolted my eyes open.

"Big!"

I jumped to my feet and flew downstairs—Father was home from the post office.

He hadn't even taken off his own hat yet, but he was holding one of my shoes.

"How did your shoes end up looking like this?"

My shoes were caked with white and gray powder, like Father's had been this morning. My coat and scarf were lightly dusted, too. I reached up and smoothed my hair; when I took my hand away, it was covered with the same grime.

"They must have—"

But my shoes wouldn't have gone anywhere on their own.

"I mean, I—"

"You disobeyed me."

"No! I—" I stepped off the bottom stair, getting closer to him. "You said not to take Kammi, and I didn't; you can ask her, she came right home."

"And you think I meant it was okay for you to go if you got rid of Kammi?"

I lowered my eyes and mumbled, "I wasn't getting around what you said. I really thought you weren't worried about me the way you were about Kammi."

"Not about what you'd see. Just physical danger. Walls can fall down hours later, or keep burning, or—"

"I know. I . . . I *saw*."

He nodded and handed me my shoe.

"Get the brush and clean these outside. Before your mother sees."

I picked up the brush and my other shoe. I stepped outside without my coat and started knocking the powder off my shoes. My breath, too, rose white in the frigid night air.

I tensed, waiting for the sirens.

# 5

*"NEEEEEOW PUD-D-D-D-D-D!"*

One of the younger boys ran circles in the schoolyard, his arms out straight like an aerial's.

"Watch it, baby!" Kaleb, an older boy, yelled at him.

"You watch it!" the smaller boy yelled back. "You watch it because I'm going to sign up for that test as soon as they let me, and then I'll fly over your house and kill you!"

Kaleb cuffed him on the head, but not too hard. "Get out of here," he said gently. The boy ran off to terrorize some girls his age, including Kammi. I hoped he wouldn't upset her. After three more nights of bombing this week, we were all tired.

"I'm going to do it for the money," one boy said. "Take the test, I mean."

"Me too," a few other boys said.

Four hundred orins . . . a family could eat on that for a year.

If there was any food to buy.

Since Tyssia and Erobern had cut our train lines to

most of the southern nations, there had been hardly any fruit. Pigs were thin because people had been eating the acorns we used to feed them. There wasn't much fat to cook in.

"My mother says signing your child up is like selling them for a currency that's going to be useless anyway when Sofarende falls," Peggi said.

A shocked silence followed her words.

Saying that out loud was treason.

I squirmed my toes inside my shoes. You could be imprisoned for treason, or even put to death. Why would Peggi's mother say such a thing in front of her? Why would Peggi repeat it?

One of the boys said, "What do you care, anyway? The test's not for girls."

"Says who? The sign says for *children* ages twelve to fourteen," Megs said. "That means boys *and* girls."

"What would they want girls for? What use are girls?"

Megs slammed her hands into his chest and knocked him over.

The other kids let up a cheer and formed a circle around them. Except for Kaleb. He leaned in and took Megs by the arm.

I stood in the middle of the circle, my heart thudding too fast.

Kaleb led Megs away by the elbow. I moved to catch up, but she turned and caught my eye. My feet stopped.

Megs looked mad.

Like she didn't want me to follow.

• • •

I took Kammi home, checked in with Mother, and walked over to Megs's house.

Something buzzed in my brain and fluttered around my heart, something that I couldn't quiet when I thought about trying to talk to her.

One of her little sisters answered the door.

"Come in, Mathilde!"

"Actually . . ." I held up my basket and looked into the house, catching Megs's mother's eye. "I was hoping Megs could come out to look for mushrooms."

Mrs. Swiller nodded. "Good idea. The soup's a bit thin tonight."

Megs looked from me to her mother; then she sighed, and got her coat and basket.

We set out to the edge of town in silence, our knitted scarves and hats bright against the gray afternoon and frosty bare trees.

Even through the frost and steam of our breath, the woods reminded me of summer, back when Megs and I could play outside for hours. When the war had seemed so far away.

I followed Megs off the path. She stooped to tug up mushrooms. Did she count each mouth as she plucked them?

She looked over at me, standing still and clutching the handle of my basket.

"Aren't you going to get any? Isn't that why you came out here?"

I knelt beside her and grabbed a couple of mushrooms, but their tops popped off into my hands, leaving behind the stumps.

"You're taking the test, aren't you?" I asked.

Megs sat back on her heels and looked at me. "I have to."

"Your mother's making you?"

"No. I just—have to."

"For the money?"

She nodded.

"Does she *want* you to take it?"

"I think she's glad she doesn't have to ask me to. That I just told her I would."

If Megs sat the test, she would get the required score, whatever it was. She was top of our class in every subject. And she'd even beaten older students in that essay contest, "Why I'm Proud to Be a Sofarender." She was working through next year's math book in the time left over in each math class when she finished her regular work early.

The sun was dropping rapidly. I stood up and pulled my coat tighter.

Megs added softly, "It could save us."

"But what if we lose *you*?"

Megs's look was steady as she stood up.

"I told you before, I don't think they'd make us do something that dangerous."

"But you don't *know* that."

"Stop it!" She stamped her foot and the mushrooms jumped in her basket, some tumbling out. "Just stop it, okay? Why do you always have to worry about everything?"

I swallowed hard as her watering eyes stared into mine.

"That's not fair." I dragged the back of my hand across my eyes, refusing to cry. "You wouldn't volunteer if you weren't worried about your family."

"You don't know what it's like! Your father's still here!"

The words hung between us. Searing.

"Still here? What about at night, during the bombings? When I don't know where he is, or if he will ever come back? You say that I worry too much, and that I don't know what it's like to worry!"

I stared at her, my heart beating fast.

But we weren't really angry at each other.

Then she nodded. She understood.

And I had to understand, too. I had to accept what she was going to do. Even though she had said she would be there with me, whatever happened, and taking the test would be breaking her promise.

I stooped, picked up the scattered mushrooms, and dropped them back into her basket. My hands were steady.

"I have to," she whispered when I stood back up.

"I know," I said.

We both crouched down and started collecting mushrooms again, though I picked as slowly as I could without making it obvious that I was leaving them for her.

The war was eating up everything—our food, our sleep, our homes, our fathers . . . now even each other.

We picked until there was nothing left in sight. Then Megs linked her arm through mine, and we were swallowed by the darkness.

# 6

A FEW NIGHTS LATER, Tye stood on a chair next to me at the kitchen sink, proud to help with the dishes, but scooping suds off the top of the water and sticking them to her chin as if she had grown a foamy white beard.

She giggled as if each time was the first time she'd thought of it.

"Come on, Tye, use those suds to clean the dishes. Here's your porridge bowl, you can clean that."

I absentmindedly rinsed the washed dishes under the running faucet and handed them to Kammi, who said, "Slow down, I can't dry them all at once."

"Oh, sorry."

"When will Mother come home?" Tye asked.

"I don't know. She went to get meat, but the line must be very long today."

"And Father?"

"He came home, didn't he?" I asked. I thought I'd heard the door open and shut a few minutes before, but wouldn't he have come in to give us our hugs?

"I think he did," Kammi said.

"You finish washing up, okay?"

Father was in the living room, hat in his lap, staring at nothing. But he sat straight up, as if he expected to hear the sirens sound at any second now that it was dark out. He had purple circles under his eyes and one of his eyelids twitched.

"Father?"

"Yes, Big?" He didn't look at me.

"When do you sleep?"

He hadn't been home in three nights. Even when we were all home, it wasn't easy to sleep; we were always waiting for the sirens, and our stomachs rumbled in the night because we were so hungry.

"When will they stop bombing us?" I asked.

He didn't answer.

"I know what's happening," I said. "You may as well talk about it. They're going to flatten us like they did the Skaves."

The many tiny kingdoms of the Skaves out east had been brutally taken by Tyssia in the past two years. At school, we'd learned that the Tyssians, who lived in rocky mountains, wanted the fertile Skaven valleys. Then the black flag of Tyssia flew over these lands, until it was replaced with the new orange and black stripes of the united Tyssia and Erobern.

Sofarende stood between Tyssia and the sea; between Tyssia and the great island nation, Eilean.

They probably wanted to sail out into the world, capture Eilean and her colonies.

Father looked up as if only just realizing that I was there.

"Oh, I'm sorry, Big, I'm sorry. Come here." He drew me into a hug.

"You think so too, then?"

"You'll have to be strong through it, whatever comes."

I nodded against his chest, his arms tight around me. But why hadn't he said *we'll* have to be strong? Us together? Wouldn't he be with me?

It was suddenly hard to breathe, but I wanted his arms to hold me even tighter, and I couldn't squeeze back nearly enough.

"If you have to go out tonight, can you stay home from the post office tomorrow?"

"I would lose the day's pay."

"But you're so tired."

Mother came home. She went to the kitchen, kissed Kammi and Tye, and put the meat she'd managed to get into the oven.

Then she came into the living room.

"Is everything all right?" she asked.

"Is anything all right?" I snapped.

Normally it wouldn't have been okay, to snap at her.

But there was no more normally.

Mother just sat down as Father let me go.

"I've been wanting the three of us to talk," she said.

In the winter, the stream out in the woods freezes, but only on top. Sometimes I punch through the ice and run my fingers in the frigid water, the cold beautifully fluid, but numbing.

That icy water was running inside my rib cage and pooling in my stomach.

"What about?"

"The army test. What do you think?" she asked Father.

He looked at both of us. Then he said carefully, "If they are screening the children, that means they aren't taking just anyone, which makes me think they aren't going to throw them away. Maybe they'll train them to have a fighting chance. Mathilde knows the enemy may make it here. She knows we're sitting ducks. Maybe we should . . . let her go."

And for the first time in my life, Father was crying.

Mother pressed her hand to her eyes.

Was the tumbling feeling inside me the same one that made Megs tell her mother she would take the test?

"Maybe . . . if I went . . . if I got it . . ." I looked at Father. "You would have money and then you wouldn't have to worry about working days at the post office. You could stay home and rest."

But my parents only cried harder.

"It's not about the money," Father said.

"No, of course not." Mother reached out to squeeze my hand, hers slippery with tears. "In fact, the money is part of what makes it so hard, because it puts a price on you."

"Then why do you want me to go?"

"I don't know that I do. I'm afraid for you to go; I'm afraid for us all to stay."

Father said, "I know that people say a family should stay together at a time like this, but I keep thinking that maybe the best chance for having at least some of the family make it is to be in different places."

*At least some of the family make it?*

The icy floods started in my chest again.

Father thought we weren't going to make it? That we were going to die?

I searched my parents' faces to see if they really believed it, but they were looking at me, waiting for me to speak.

How could I leave them?

How could they send me away?

"I . . . I don't think I can pass it. I'd be the youngest. So I don't see . . ."

I had been going to say "the harm in trying," but Mother jumped in as if she assumed I'd been about to say "why I should try."

"Oh, no, no, no, honey, it will be okay if you don't, I just don't want you to miss your opportunity because we were afraid to try it."

"It could save you," Father said.

"It could kill me."

Mother twisted her hands in her lap. Father had tears leaking out of his eyes.

No one said that it wasn't true.

Finally, Father said, "They promise university educations. They wouldn't if they didn't expect the children to make it to them."

"It's an easier promise if they don't expect them to," Mother said, so quietly it gave me chills. "But you're right, why would they select them so carefully, train them for something, and then throw them away?"

Her voice sounded like Megs's. Reasonable. Hoping. Almost pleading.

But Megs had a chance to pass. She was closer to the older kids in her studies. I couldn't catch up in two weeks.

But if agreeing to the test would give Mother and Father two weeks of hope, then that would be worth it.

I got up and left the living room. When I returned, they were both staring at me. They probably thought I'd walked out because I was upset.

But my eyes were dry, my hands steady, as I held out the form to Mother.

"You'll both need to sign."

Mother read it carefully, though she must have many times already; probably Father had, too. "When you sign, though," I reminded them, "it means if I pass, I have to do whatever they say. We decide now, not later."

I felt like I was the adult, reminding them that choices can have consequences we can't even begin to understand.

Father moved first, but slowly. He patted his pockets.

And took out a pen.

He signed, and passed the pen to Mother.

She held it for a minute.

Then she signed, too.

Father handed the form back to me. Mother stood, touched my head gently, and gave me a kiss. "I'm going to go check on dinner."

I nodded. Father followed her, leaving me staring at the document in my hands, at my parents' signatures giving away the rest of my childhood.

Maybe my whole life.

No matter.

I folded the paper back up.

# 7

IN THE MORNING, I stood by Miss Tameron's desk.

"Yes, Mathilde?"

I handed her the form.

She went still.

"You all talked about it, as a family?"

"Yes."

She studied me, rubbing one chalky-white hand with the other as if cold. But after a moment, she seemed to think of something else, and smiled.

"That's all right, Mathilde. It will be all right."

I nodded, and went back to my seat.

Megs looked over at me, her eyebrows raised.

I nodded.

Then her eyes narrowed, and she started scribbling her math assignment with dark, noisy pencil marks.

I swallowed hard, and tried to do my own assignment.

But when Miss Tameron rang her little bell for our morning break, Megs stood silently by my desk while I pretended to concentrate on my work.

"You coming? I got your coat and scarf."

I looked up, taking my clothes from her like a hug. She stayed close as I put them on.

She smiled. "Come on, silly."

And we went outside together.

"Mathilde? I'm sorry to interrupt your work, but could you watch Tye while I make dinner?"

I shut my book with relief. I'd spent the past several afternoons stuck at my desk, under Mother's orders to prepare for the test.

"I don't think they played outside today. She has a lot of energy," Mother said.

I followed her downstairs, where Tye was leaping between the sofa and the chairs.

"She's been running through the kitchen. With the boiling water . . ."

"I can watch her."

The best trick to get Tye to stop whatever she was doing was to do something fun without her.

I got out our can of crayons and a few sheets of paper—our last sheets, actually. Paper was getting scarce.

But it seemed like an okay time to use it.

I spread a sheet out on the floor in the living room and lay on my stomach, tipping over the can of crayons.

Crayons were a treasure, too. Our small collection was all mismatched stubs.

Tye was still jumping around me as I selected a green crayon and started drawing a large circle.

"What are you doing?"

"Homework. Serious stuff."

I continued to draw.

"Can I help?"

"Oh, probably not. It's *really* hard."

"Not too hard for me."

"Well, I have to draw a picture of our house."

"Our house isn't a circle. And it's not green."

"Oh." I stopped. "What would you do, then?"

She sighed and shoved me out of the way, picked beige crayons, and started drawing squares and rectangles.

I sighed, too, as she settled and started drawing a pony outside of our house.

Not that we had a pony.

Kammi came home from her friend's house. "What are you doing?" she asked.

"Mathilde's homework," Tye said.

Kammi looked at me, about to ask, but I shook my head.

"You know what would be really fun?" Kammi asked. "If we could use the paints."

"Why *don't* we?" I asked. "They'll only dry up and go to waste. We can finish the paints and paper together. Let's just go upstairs so we're not in Mother's way."

Tye scooped up the papers and took them upstairs while Kammi put away the crayons. I found the paint tubes and brushes, and squeezed the colors into a tin. Red, green, yellow, blue.

The girls each painted a picture. When I went to refresh the paints for them, the tubes felt all squeezed out.

But there was only one more piece of paper anyway.

"Let's do our handprints," I said.

My sisters giggled as I brushed rainbow swirls of paint onto their hands. I pressed Tye's onto the center of the paper. Then Kammi's outside that. They both held up their hands, grinning. I painted my left hand, and Kammi took the brush to paint my right. My bigger prints joined theirs on the paper, on the outside, sheltering them.

Little, Middle, and Big.

The handprints looked like they belonged to one person who was growing, captured a few years apart.

I pinned it to the wall. My sisters stood back, admiring. We ignored the fingerprint smudges I'd made at the corners of the paper and on the wall, even though we were never allowed to color on the walls.

"It's beautiful," Tye said.

And it was.

Still holding our hands in the air, we looked sadly at the remaining paint in the tin.

"I wish we could paint more," Tye said. And then she pressed her entire hand into the paints.

"Tye!" Kammi cried.

Warmth pressed on the inside of my ribs, way up high, by my heart.

"Do the other one," I said.

Kammi's mouth fell open, but Tye removed her hand and pressed the other into the paint.

I climbed onto the chair and then onto the desk, and signaled to Tye to follow me, which she did, carefully, her hands still raised.

She pressed her palms and then her fingers spread wide against the white wall.

"Kammi?" I asked.

I couldn't tell them that our house would be turned to rubble any night now. What did the walls matter?

What mattered is that we were standing here right now, the three of us together.

Kammi dipped her hands and pressed them to the wall.

I did mine.

And then we were laughing, and we couldn't stop. We stood on my bed and pressed the wall there.

Then the slanted eves.

In a row under the window.

When our house was knocked down, and someone picked through its pieces, maybe he would find these handprints, and know that children had lived here.

That *we* had lived here.

And if our house turned to dust, then within the dust would be a million tiny particles with our stamp. The universe would remember we had existed.

My sisters stopped giggling.

I turned.

Mother stood in the doorway.

The warmth in my chest reached a squeezing heat.

"We—I . . ."

Mother came into the room, turning slowly. Her brow was creased again. Was she deciding how angry to be?

Then her face relaxed, and she folded me into a hug, kissed my cheek.

"I love it."

"You do?"

I looked up, surprised to see tears gathering in her eyes.

"My only worry is how much soap we'll use cleaning you up."

"Oh."

I looked down at my hands.

I hadn't thought about soap.

"Go ahead, now. Help your sisters. Dinner's ready."

# 8

"GIRLS, WAKE UP. Mathilde, it's testing day."

My sisters threw on their school clothes and hurried down-stairs to eat, but my fingers felt cold as I did up my buttons.

I sat in front of my breakfast so long that eventually Mother sat down next to me. I picked up my spoon and ate a few mouthfuls.

"It's time to go," she said at last. She kissed my temple. "Good luck."

I went to the front hall and found my coat. Those buttons gave me trouble, too.

"Listen, Big."

Father pulled me aside in the doorway. I hugged him, clinging like a toddler on the first day of kindercare.

Finally he managed to hold me at arm's length. He crouched down. "What is it?" he asked, as gently as he would have spoken to Tye.

But I pressed into his chest again and mumbled, "My frid may von't elth mm go."

"Oh." He chuckled. "They'll let you go. They have to score the tests. That takes time." He patted his pockets.

I drew back at last, and he stood up.

He pulled three copper coins from his shirt pocket and gestured for me to hold out my hand, which I did, not believing it when he set the coins there. Each was worth just an eighth of an orin, but was a treasure in our house.

"No matter what happens, you're worth a million orins to me. A million times a million, then times all the stars in the sky ... though I don't have a million orins, so you can have the coppers I do have. For the baker's on the way home—get yourself a treat, when it's over. However it goes, I'm very proud of you for signing up."

Three coppers ... I could buy a glazed bun or a tiny sweet cake. All for myself.

What would we go without later so that I could have this treat?

No, not later: Father hadn't had toast this morning, just coffee.

And no bread with his soup last night.

"Thank you, Father." I flopped in for one more hug. "I love you."

"And I love you, Big. Go on now, Kammi's getting ahead and you don't want to be late today."

I nodded, and tucked the coins inside my coat pocket. Father straightened my scarf and tugged my braids free, and then I was flying up the street after my sister.

In the schoolyard, the younger children ran around like there was no food shortage and no war and their fathers weren't away and their houses not knocked down.

But we older ones lingered, unusually still, whether we were taking the test or not.

My heart longed to run around with the younger children, but my legs felt too wobbly. Megs and I stood together, watching our breath turn to steam in the air.

"That must be the Examiner," Megs whispered.

I looked over at the teachers. The new woman had dull blond hair pulled into a tight knot at the nape of her neck. She wore a gray army uniform with a jacket and a skirt to her knees.

Kammi ran over and tugged my sleeve.

"Mathilde!" She squeezed my arm.

"Ouch! What?" I asked. "What's wrong?"

"Jullen says they're taking everybody today, everybody who sits the test. If you signed the papers, you belong to the army already!"

"That isn't true," Megs said. "If they were taking everybody, they wouldn't be holding a test, would they?"

The bell rang.

Megs ran to the line for the test, not wanting to lose points for tardiness.

But when I looked down at Kammi, she was crying.

"Hey, shh . . ." I knelt to look into her eyes. Her worry was the same one I'd confessed to Father. "Megs is right, they won't take people who won't be useful. I don't have much of a chance to be picked."

Kammi frowned at me, doubtful.

"I'm nowhere near the top of my class, and most of the kids are two years older than me. Miss Tameron seemed surprised I'm even going to sit the test, but anyone's allowed to."

Kammi scowled, still not believing me.

The yard had almost cleared. We didn't have much time.

"Listen, you'll get out of school hours before me today. Get a treat." I put the coins in her hand.

Her mouth dropped open as she turned them over.

"Where did you get these?"

"Father."

Suddenly I felt warmer, lighter. Father had said he would be proud no matter how I did. And if he was scrimping on bread, he wasn't expecting the four hundred orins.

He wasn't expecting me to pass.

What a gift Father had given me in these coins!

I glanced up at the teachers. The Examiner was staring at me from the head of the testing line, brow creased and mouth set straight.

Uh-oh.

I jumped, grabbed Kammi's hand and ran her over to her line, and hurried to the back of my line.

The Examiner asked, "Mathilde Joss?"

Process of elimination: I was the last one.

"Yes."

"You're late."

"Yes."

"Care to explain yourself?"

"No."

She nodded and entered a mark on her attendance sheet.

I swallowed hard and stared solemnly back at her.

The Examiner's assistant led us to a large classroom. At each of the forty desks sat two booklets, a pink one with printed text and a blank blue book, plus two sharp pencils.

The Examiner had somehow gotten there ahead of us, as

if she could evaporate and reappear in a different place. She said, "You will sit in alphabetical order by last name, starting in the front left, one behind the other."

Then she called our names and we took our seats. Some of the older students, especially the boys, were much taller than me. I felt very small in my chair.

Megs sat behind me to the right. I turned to look at her, but she was so focused that I couldn't catch her eye. She was like that during tests. I turned back around.

The Examiner said, "Put your lunch pails on the floor. Verify that your name is on the pink booklet in front of you."

Mine was.

"And on the answer booklet."

Mine was.

"Many of your answers will go into the pink booklets, but for math problems and longer paragraph answers, you may use the answer booklet. You may work in any order, but make sure to number the answers you enter in the blank book. You have all day today, but not any longer. There will be a break at noon for lunch and stretching."

She paused, but no one moved. No one would dare open the booklets before being instructed to.

The Examiner's manner changed, from being someone who looked like she would take a ruler to us for the slightest infraction to someone who might, maybe, give a crying child a hug.

Maybe.

"Before you begin, I want to thank you for volunteering to serve your country. You are very young, and, if selected, you may spend the rest of your childhoods away from home.

None of you have taken the decision to be here lightly. Nor have your families. All of Sofarende appreciates your willingness."

She looked each of us in the eye in turn.

Then she became stern again.

"There is to be no talking. If you need to use the washroom, raise your hand, and my assistant will escort you in silence. Otherwise, no one who leaves will be permitted to return.

"You may open your booklets and begin."

A quick flutter of paper as forty booklets were opened at the same time; cracks of the booklets' spines being creased to lie open; taps of pencils being removed from the grooves in the desks. I glanced around the room, but when my eyes looked forward the Examiner was watching me again, so I cleared my throat and opened my own pink booklet.

Fifty pages crammed full of tiny, typed text. I turned through the pages, slowly. Enough work for a day, or two, even for a grown-up.

It probably wasn't possible to finish the test today.

We wouldn't be expected to.

Phew.

I settled on pages with math I knew, opened the blank blue book, and got to work.

After the math, I moved on to translations. They seemed to expect us to know every language on the Continent, and those from Eilean and Nor'land, too! I thought I understood most of the passages, and scribbled out everything I could.

I was surprised when the Examiner announced, "Please close your booklets. You may stretch, walk around this room, and eat, but you are still not permitted to talk."

I stretched, got my lunch pail, and looked to Megs. We walked over to the wall and sat together.

I opened my lunch pail to find that Father hadn't been the only one who'd wanted me to have treats today. My slice of bread, packed by Mother, had a paper-thin spread of butter and, even more unbelievable, a sprinkle of sugar. There was also a small, beautifully shined, green apple.

Megs's sandwich had an extra slice of spicy red sausage on it. Extra meat was even more special than my sprinkle of sugar.

I pulled my sweater more tightly around my middle and leaned against Megs.

Megs sat straight and stiff. She took tiny bites, chewing carefully.

Halfway through my sugared bread, I held it out to her. She shook her head. Halfway through my apple, I held that out to her, too. She shook her head again, but I continued holding out the apple. She took two bites and handed it back.

The Examiner's attendant came by and offered us each a glass of water and a trip to the washroom. The Examiner, while keeping a close eye on everyone, set two new pencils on every desk, taking the dull ones away. Where a student had worn out the erasers in the morning, she left an extra pink cube eraser for the afternoon.

Megs and I stayed together against the wall, and I squeezed her hand.

She would do fine. She would be picked to go.

Though if this was how nervous she was on testing day, what about all the days that would follow? When she was serving in the war?

When Megs went, she would go without me.

# 9

THE TEST BECAME MORE and more peculiar as I flipped through the pages.

About ten pages had blank maps to fill in.

A map of the Continent was labeled for the current year. Since borders had been shifting with the advance of Tyssia, I added last month before the year. I shaded all of the Skaven lands as part of Tyssia. I named the southern states, the small countries to the west and south of Erobern that blocked their sea access, as best I could.

A map of the whole world was labeled THE GREATEST HISTORICAL EXTENT OF SOFARENDE. I shaded in most of where we are now with more Tyssian provinces included, and then the colonies all over the world.

We didn't have colonies anymore. We'd given them up, granted freedom to those lands, and focused on life at home.

After the maps were questions or instructions:

*Describe the origins of Sofarende.*

All of us knew that. The ancient and medieval Eileans and Nor'landers and Sofarers sailed to each other's lands and blended, so that Sofarenders were descended from those peoples, too. We spread into southern parts of Sofarende, like where we lived, that were more mountainous, and mixed with the mountain peoples there, too, the peoples who on other mountains became Tyssians or Erobins. We were strong because we were made of everyone. All the provinces voted to be one country, under one seafarer flag, a hundred years ago.

*How did the current war come about?*

I jotted down how Tyssia had taken the Skaven kingdoms, one by one. Sofarende and Eilean had pledged to defend the Skaves if anything like that happened, so we had to fight. Then Tyssia joined with Erobern and started attacking us.

Next came pages and pages of patterns—numerical, geometric, lyrical, musical—without directions. I continued each or wrote down what I noticed.

Then there was a whole page that was a jumble of letters, like a word-find puzzle. I circled some words I found in the lines, but I didn't know if I could look backward and diagonally, too, or change direction midword, or if I could just use the jumble of letters to create words. So I just circled words every which way until the paper was crammed full of circles, and then I started listing on the side. I concentrated so hard I forgot I was taking a test.

I turned the page and went completely still.

*326) How do aerials stay up?*

*327) When flying at 10,000 feet and 350 miles per hour toward a target with a load to drop, when should you drop the load to hit the target?*

Was this what the whole test was about after all?

*Were* they looking for kids to fly aerials?

Were these the only questions in this whole booklet that mattered?

I didn't want to fly aerials. I didn't want to drop bombs on people.

I looked at the first question again. I had no idea what kept aerials up. So I just wrote, "Engines. Propellers. Wings. Air pressure."

As for the second question, I didn't know how to do those kinds of calculations. I figured that the load would be moving forward, like the aerial itself, so I wrote, "Before you get there."

Suddenly Kaleb got up, his chair scraping loudly on the wooden floor. He walked to the front of the room, handed in his booklets, and left.

We stared after him.

In the next few minutes, other boys started handing in their exams, too. Maybe they had just been waiting for someone to be brave enough to go first.

How had they decided they were done? Had they answered everything they knew? Or were they just tired of answering?

I didn't think I had answered enough yet. As I flipped through the remaining pages, the questions became more and more random.

*Draw and label a sound fortress.*

That was actually something I *could* do, though I wondered which country's features they wanted me to use. I decided the key word was *sound*. I could pull from any tradition, as long as it made a good fortress.

Hmm.

I drew.

*You are packing a picnic lunch for a friend. What do you include?*

What was this? A chance to show that I knew proper nutrition? Then why wouldn't they ask for a whole week's meals?

Bread, meat, cheese, fruit . . .

Then something else occurred to me, so I wrote, "That depends on what my friend likes to eat."

Suddenly someone was crying. From a few seats back and to my right.

Megs.

She flew up the aisle and out the door.

She wouldn't be allowed back in.

That was the rule.

I ran into the hallway. "Megs?"

I found her down the hall, back against the wall, knees drawn up. The Examiner's assistant approached her, but when she heard my footsteps, she paused. She nodded at me and returned to the classroom door. The Examiner poked her head into the hallway, saw me crouching down to talk to Megs, gave me a stern, searching look, and shut the door.

We were officially done with the test.

Relief washed through me, warm as sunshine.

But Megs . . .

She had her arms drawn up over her head, which was resting on her knees.

I put a hand on her shoulder, but she flinched and drew in her breath as if burned.

"Megs, it's just me."

She was crying too hard to answer, so I sat down next to her.

Finally Megs said, "What am I going to tell Mother? What will she say? She's going to be so disappointed. I couldn't finish it. I tried and tried, but it was like I would never finish."

How had she not seen?

"You weren't meant to finish. No one was."

She looked at me through her fingers. "Really? Why didn't *I* notice that?"

"You were probably . . . so focused you didn't see it. I bet you still did great. I bet you answered enough to show how smart you are."

"You really think that's possible?"

"Of course I do. I bet everything you wrote down was . . . was perfect."

Something caught in my throat and I stopped talking.

Megs stopped crying and looked up. My being unable to continue was to Megs what Father's saving for the coins had been to me. His saving confirmed that he thought I wouldn't make it. My crying confirmed that I believed she *would* go.

She would go, and I would never see her again.

Miss Tameron walked down the hallway.

"All done, girls?" Her eyes scanned our red, puffy ones.

We nodded.

"That's a relief, then?"

We nodded.

"Have a good night. I'll be glad to have you back tomorrow. No one wanted to answer my questions without you, Megs. Oh, Mathilde, did you know you have blue paint on your ear?"

I reached up to feel both of my ears; they must have glowed pink with my embarrassment.

"Good night, girls."

"Good night, Miss Tameron."

Megs seemed calmer. I stood in front of her, presenting both hands, and she took them. Hers were still wet with tears. Hard to hold on to as she stood up.

At dinner, Kammi pushed her chair close to mine. We kept bumping elbows as we cut our meat and carrots. When Mother turned to get something from the stove, I poured half of my milk into Kammi's glass.

"How was it, Big?"

"Hmm?"

What was the best thing to say? That I'd walked out of the test, to follow Megs, when maybe I could have done more?

They probably wouldn't be too impressed by that.

"I answered a lot of questions."

"What kinds of things did they ask you?" Father asked.

"Math, translations, patterns . . ."

"So you think it went well?" Mother asked.

"You let me go with blue paint on my ear."

"It suited you," Mother said. The corners of her mouth twitched into a smile; suddenly Father and I were smiling, too.

The glowing candlelight—no electricity tonight— seemed to flicker inside me as well, warm and soothing.

A shred of darkness remained, like that creeping in through the windows between the curtains.

Megs would be going away.

# 10

THREE DAYS LATER, the entire school was called to an assembly at the end of the day. The teachers tried to hush us, to make us face forward.

Then the Examiner marched in and we fell silent.

"I am here to announce the results of the Aptitude Test, which many of you sat just a few days ago. We very much appreciate the willingness of each student. From this group, I have selected one for service."

Megs's hand, which had been pressed into mine, went slack. I tried to hold on.

"Please offer your congratulations to . . ." The Examiner looked around, trying to locate her winner. Her victim.

"Mathilde Joss."

Megs's hand finally slipped out of mine.

Everyone was still and quiet.

A hand touched my shoulder. "This way, Mathilde." Miss Tameron guided me to the door of the hall as students moved up the aisle around me.

"Congratulations, Mathilde."

"Congratulations."

But it didn't sound like congratulations. It sounded heavier. Like they weren't happy. Or wobbly. Like they were scared.

Scared for my life?

That was it. My life had ended. I'd stopped breathing. My heart had stopped beating, when the Examiner had said my name.

Megs had been next to me, but where was she? When had we been separated? And Kammi? She'd been in the room, too. Why hadn't she come to find me?

The Examiner waited for me in the principal's office, alone. I sat, legs numb and fingers tingly.

"Congratulations, Mathilde. You should be very proud." She sat in the principal's chair.

I looked down at my lap.

"Aren't you?" When I didn't answer, she said, "You can't back out. You've signed the papers, as have your parents. Your service is compulsory."

Her misunderstanding my silence helped me find my voice.

"I— There's been a mistake."

"A mistake? You mean, you made a mistake in signing up for the test? In signing those papers?"

"No. There's been a mistake in the test."

"Oh?"

"Yes. If only one student has passed, it must . . . it would have to be Megs, not me."

"Oh," she repeated, in a very different tone. "Why's that?"

"Megs, she's ... she's the top of the class, always. I've never beaten her at an exam. Ever. I couldn't have beaten her at this one, either."

"Hmm. Logic. I see." The Examiner settled back, as if pleased with our conversation now. "Consider, you used the word *always*. Was this test like any that you had taken before?"

"Well, no."

"So, if the test was different this time, would it mean that you still couldn't beat her?"

I bit my lip.

"I helped design the test, and I evaluate it. I saw in yours—in you—the qualities I was looking for."

"But not in Megs?"

She cleared her throat. "I shouldn't discuss another student's results with you, but you may realize that the way Megs left wasn't helpful to her score."

"But—I—we left at the same time."

She nodded. "At the same time, yes. But for very different reasons."

I didn't see the difference.

I twisted the hem of my skirt in my lap. "Can you ... take her instead? Her family needs this more."

The Examiner smiled, as if I had proven something to her. "No. I chose you. I still choose you."

I sighed.

"Well, if you want me, can't you *also* take Megs?"

"Lucky for you, when this war is over and you are the right age, we will be paying for your university education. You can study law and argue all day if you so desire."

That meant no.

"Any other questions?"

"Can I go now? My sister, she's been afraid of this. . . . She'll be upset."

"Yes. But you'll have a little more time to spend with her. I'll come by tonight and meet your family."

She paused as I stood, as if expecting something more. I remembered her congratulations, as if I'd been awarded an honor. She would be paying my family now, and providing me with food, shelter, an education.

If I lived to get it.

"Thank you," I said stiffly.

She nodded, and I left.

# 11

MOTHER STOOD IN front of our house, wringing a dish towel, as if she'd been holding it when she heard and never let go.

Father should have been at the post office, but he was there, holding his arms open.

I ran to him. He picked me up, held me, my head on his shoulder, like I was still his Little.

Like I would always be his Little.

Neighbors stared in silence, lips pressed straight.

Even Mrs. Heller had nothing to say.

It wasn't every day that a girl of twelve was sent to war.

Mother let Tye play in the kitchen with the real tea set. The one that had been Mother's mother's mother's.

The one that would have been mine.

"You'll stay here with Tye," Mother told Kammi.

"But I want to hear!" Kammi's voice and hands trembled. I hadn't been able to find her after school; she, like Megs, hadn't waited for me. Kammi had run home and sat in her bed, not even removing her coat until Mother did it for her.

"You can listen, we'll leave the door open," Mother said.

She filled the teapot with water, and Father gave each of the girls half a slice of bread for making pretend cakes or biscuits. He caught my eye as he handed out these treats. They would have money for more, now. Maybe they could even have real cakes *and* real biscuits.

I sat in a chair in the corner, watching. I didn't belong to them anymore.

Mother came and put her hand on my cheek.

"Come to the living room, love."

I nodded and followed her as the doorbell rang. Father went to answer.

"Good evening, Mr. Joss. I presume you know why I've come?"

"Yes, yes, good evening. Come in."

The worn wood floor creaked as she stepped inside.

"Can I take your coat?" Father asked. "Would you like some tea or water?"

"No, thank you." The Examiner came into the living room, still in her coat. She wouldn't be staying long, then. "Mrs. Joss, Mathilde."

Mother rose. "Welcome, please sit."

The Examiner took the free chair.

My parents sat on either side of me on the sofa, Mother's hand on my knee, Father's on my shoulder. I thought about their gentle pressure until I realized the Examiner had been talking and I wasn't listening.

"I'm pleased to inform you, in person, that Mathilde has been selected for service. It's quite an honor, and all of Sofarende is grateful to her and to you. Mathilde is not only the only pupil in her school, but the only pupil in the city of Lykkelig, whom I have selected. Do you know why, Mathilde?"

"No."

"No matter." To my parents, she said, "She did very well on her Aptitude Test."

Mother nodded; Father remained still.

"We did want this for her," Mother said. "We wouldn't have signed her up otherwise. But I can't say it hasn't come as a bit of a shock, to learn she'll really be going."

The Examiner nodded. "You must have many questions. To discuss some practical matters first, you are to put Mathilde on the two-thirteen p.m. train the day after tomorrow."

"Alone?" Mother asked.

"Yes. The train crew will have been alerted to her presence. You needn't worry."

Mother nodded, looking, if possible, somewhat more shocked.

"She will be considered military personnel, but we do not typically ask the children to be in uniform if they already have adequate clothing."

"She has her school clothes," Mother said.

"Those will do perfectly. Pack her clothing in a suitcase she can carry. We also encourage the children to bring a small memento from home, perhaps a family photograph or a stuffed toy. It helps them with their homesickness, especially as"—she cleared her throat—"they won't be allowed any communications in or out once they arrive."

My parents stiffened.

"That's necessary?" Father asked.

"Yes. For their safety and military secrecy. You will receive monthly notification of her continued wellness."

No more Father and Mother.

No more Kammi and Tye.

No more Megs.

"While her whereabouts will be a secret, you can rest assured that no children will be sent to the front. I can promise her safety to that extent, but I cannot guarantee that we won't be bombed."

Father nodded. "The same as here."

"Precisely."

"When will she be allowed home?" Mother asked.

"Because of the confidential nature of her work, that will be when we see fit to release her; expect it to be after the end of the conflict."

"And we don't know when that will be," Mother said softly.

"Perhaps not until she's grown up," Father said, even more softly. "But maybe this will give her that chance."

The Examiner nodded. "I hope so. Our bomb shelter is under concrete and steel, which is more than we can say for those of most civilian homes, unfortunately."

She handed my father an envelope. He opened it. It was stuffed full of paper bills: four hundred orins. He looked at the money sadly.

He had said that I was worth more to him than that.

"Inside the envelope is the address of the military office a few blocks from here where you can go for your family's weekly pay; you will need to show identification. We've included a few other backup addresses in case something happens to that office."

No one said anything about where to go if something happened to all the offices. Maybe they'd just be glad to think I had food and somewhere to sleep.

Assuming those things were true.

"Is there anything else you'd like to know?"

What was there to ask? Location: secret. Work: confidential.

Mother took my hand and asked the Examiner, "Will you be there with the children?"

"When I'm not recruiting or on a mission, I'll be on-site, yes. We have a large staff who helps look after them. I'll leave you to enjoy these last days together. I know this is . . . difficult, but we all must do what we can in these times, and this is a great opportunity for Mathilde. It really is. You should be very proud of her achievement and of how you've raised her."

She probably hadn't expected a family numb with dread, but excited and relieved.

Who could say which was the right way to feel?

After Father had seen her out, he sat with me while Mother took my sisters up for their bath.

"Do you want anything?" Father asked cautiously. "Big?"

"Megs," I said.

"It's late. After dark. The curfew. You can't go out."

"You can," I whispered through the lump in my throat.

Father thought, then stood up. "I'll be right back."

He went upstairs and returned in his street patrol outfit. I ran and hugged him.

"Get your coat."

He gave me his arm and we set out for Megs's house.

When I knocked on the Swillers' door, her mother opened it.

"Mathilde!"

"May Mathilde visit Megs for an hour?" Father asked.

She nodded. "I'll get Megs." While I waited, Father walked home.

Megs appeared with crossed arms and a steely look.

"Hi," I said.

"Hello."

We stood there.

"It wasn't my fault," I managed.

She uncrossed her arms. "I know. Come in?"

I followed her to her attic bedroom. She shut the door and we sat on her bed. Then she hugged me for a long time. I let myself go limp and just be held.

"I'm sorry," I sighed.

"About what?"

"That they picked me and not you. I tried to tell the Examiner that it should have been you. Or that they should also take you." And then I whispered, "I never thought you wouldn't be going."

"It was dumb to sign up if you weren't willing to go alone." She let go and stepped over to the tiny window above the desk.

"It's not that I'm not willing. I just didn't think it could happen that way." She didn't turn. "I won't be allowed to write to you."

She remained still, staring out the window. "You know, at night, when the sirens go off, if I take just a minute, I can see the aerials from here."

"Is that why you're always late?"

"I just want to know what we're hiding from," she said, echoing my own words.

"Anything out there?"

"Not yet."

She headed back to me and sat down, but so we weren't touching. My fingers played with the fringe on her bedspread.

"Do you think they're going to make us fly aerials?" I asked.

"That would be smart, wouldn't it? You'd need less fuel and you could go faster with a crew half the weight of grown men." Megs leaned back against the wall, as if we were just talking about homework.

"You answered the questions about the aerials, didn't you? I mean, you used details and number calculations?"

"Of course. *You* must have."

But I hadn't.

*Why* would they have picked me over her?

"You *really* think they'll have us flying aerials?"

"I don't know."

"Then what do you think they want children to do?"

"Something only children can do."

"But I can't do anything."

Megs moved closer to me again, and looked me in the eyes when she said, "Maybe there's something *only* you can do."

# 12

TYE AND KAMMI SHRIEKED with laughter as Father made a boiled egg disappear, only to reappear moments later. Tye flipped his hands over after each disappearance to confirm that the egg wasn't there.

We never had eggs. And Father was treating this one like a toy.

"No school for you this morning." Mother set a plate of toast in front of me. She set down a second plate of soft cheese. I hadn't seen cheese like that since before the war. She squeezed my shoulder. "Eat."

"Why no school?"

"You can go this afternoon to say goodbye to everyone."

I coated my bread with cheese. It was both tart and sweet, the way I remembered it. I pushed the cheese plate to the center of the table to share it.

Kammi headed to school with Eliza Heller, the way she would every day without me. Father left a few minutes later in his post office uniform, holding Tye's hand, taking her to kindercare. In Tye's other hand was the boiled egg. She kept looking at it, wondering if it would disappear. If it didn't, it would be her lunch.

Did she know how to peel it?

"Come," Mother said, putting on her coat with a swoosh.

Outside, she took my hand like Father had held Tye's.

The first store we tried to go to was on a bombed street, so we walked a few more blocks to another shop.

My cheeks grew hot with embarrassment as we went inside and were surrounded by girls' underthings.

It was just like Mother to worry about *underthings* at a time like this.

"Can I help you?" the shop-lady asked.

"Yes. I'd like three warm slips, three warm undershirts and three light ones, and six pairs of panties, all in her size."

"Let me measure you," the shop-lady said to me.

I let her, and then she looked through stacks of labeled cardboard boxes. "Special occasion?" she asked.

I think what she meant was: *It's unusual for a family to spend so much money on underwear right now. Not that I mind.*

"Mathilde is going away," Mother explained.

"Ah. Off to family up north? Other children are being sent. It's safer farther from the border, they say."

"No. She's passed the army test."

The shop-lady paused. "She has? And you're letting her go?"

"We had hoped they would have a place for her."

The lady slid several opened boxes toward Mother across the counter. "You have your choice." Mother looked them over as the lady went on. "I don't know that I'd be able to separate from one of my own. Send her off into the army to do who knows what."

Mother bit her lip. Did she really want to give this woman her money?

But there wasn't another shop.

Mother made her choices. Then she said, "I want another set in the next size." She looked at me, then back at the shop-lady. "She'll grow."

We walked slowly through the streets, each with a box of new clothes in hand.

"Why did she try to make you feel bad?" I asked.

"Sometimes . . ." Mother searched for the right words. "Sometimes when people don't have an opportunity, they have to convince themselves that they wouldn't have wanted it anyway."

"But why did she have to say that to you?"

"She's scared. Everyone is. I have to trust that I'm doing the right thing for you. And she has to trust that she's doing the right thing for her children."

"But still, why did she have to *say* that?"

"It helps her, to say it out loud."

"But it hurt you. Did she *want* to hurt you?"

"She was protecting herself. It is easy to protect yourself and your loved ones; it is harder to protect and care about others."

I thought about that. "But—"

"You have a lot of buts, Mathilde."

"Good thing you bought me all these panties."

And then we were both laughing, and Mother drew me to her.

• • •

Mother dropped me off at school with my lunch pail. A large banner stretched across the front of my classroom: WE'LL MISS YOU, MATHILDE!

I froze in the doorway. But Miss Tameron smiled and Megs came to get me, taking my hand and drawing me inside.

Miss Tameron set out a plate of little cakes sweetened with dried fruit. "Help yourselves," she said. The class took cakes and formed little clusters to talk. But I stayed apart from everyone.

Miss Tameron waved to me, and I went up to her desk.

"I wish you all the best, Mathilde," she said. "I hope the world is good to you. And that you are good to the world."

I nodded, though I didn't know what she meant.

"Visit with the others. Say your goodbyes."

I drifted back to Megs at our desks.

A boy named Stev came over to me. "Why are we celebrating *you*? Here's what I think of *you*." He crushed his cake to crumbs all over my desk.

How could he wreck that lovely little cake? How much time and money had it cost Miss Tameron?

Megs jumped at him, toppling the desk between them. Miss Tameron hurried over and pulled Megs off Stev.

"Miss Swiller. Miss Joss. Take a walk."

She was punishing me at my own farewell party?

Megs marched to the door.

"Your coats and hats, girls. Your lunch pails."

She meant more than a cool-off walk.

We collected our things.

Miss Tameron stepped into the hall with us.

"Stev ruined your little cake," I told her.

"Oh, Mathilde . . . I don't care about the cake." She knelt and hugged me. She held me gently, and for a very long time, not like a teacher, but like Mother.

We went to the woods.

"What about your lessons?" I asked Megs.

"Don't be ridiculous."

We found a spot we liked. Megs spread her clean handkerchief on the ground and we unpacked our lunches onto it: a winter picnic. Megs smiled, and from her pocket she pulled two of Miss Tameron's little cakes.

"Clever," I said.

"Thanks."

I wanted so much to enjoy the cake, but my mouth felt dry.

"Are you scared?"

"Maybe."

"Sad?"

"Maybe?"

"What *can* you tell me?"

I swallowed, the closest to tears I had been since the Examiner called my name.

Maybe I shouldn't tell her. I had to practice not telling her things. We'd already started, a little.

But she was Megs. *My* Megs.

For just one more day.

"They're taking us away from each other. We can't be friends anymore. Not even in letters."

"Mathilde. We will *always* be friends. *Always.* Here. Call me." She closed her eyes.

"What?" I almost laughed.

"In your mind."

I closed my eyes. *Megs?*

*Megs?*

I peeked an eye open, to see she was doing the same.

"Did you . . . ?"

"No. Try from here." She leaned across our picnic, and pressed her hand to my breastbone.

I nodded, and she pulled her hand away.

I closed my eyes.

I tried not to use words. I tried not to picture.

Hundreds of walks to school, and almost as many back home. Hundreds of summer days. Splashing in the stream. Snowball fights and forts. Braids that had started chin-length and had grown past shoulders. Shared lunches. Snacks. Stories. Smiles. Secrets. Whispers. Walks. Today.

Eyes still closed, I found the girl sitting across from me. Felt her out.

When I opened my eyes at last, hers were still closed, leaking tears.

But as if she knew my eyes were open, she nodded.

# 13

I OPENED THE SUITCASE Father had given me and set my things inside: school blouses and skirts, nightclothes, new underthings, tights, and socks.

They hardly filled the space. Not even halfway.

The Examiner had said to bring one personal item from home. I looked around our bedroom.

"Did you forget something?" Kammi turned to look around, too.

"It's empty," Tye announced, and checked my dresser drawer. Then she opened the bottom drawer, where we kept the sheets, scooped up an armful, carried it toward me—leaving a trail of cloth stretched across the bedroom—and dropped it into the suitcase.

I laughed and scooped them back out. "Thank you, but I don't think I'll need them."

"Won't you have a bed?"

"They didn't say to bring sheets, so they must have them there for us."

*Would* we have beds and sheets? Army cots? Sleeping bags? Would we be move around a lot, or stay in one place?

How would I sleep without my sisters nearby? I was used to their breathing, their warmth.

And then I knew what to bring.

They didn't object as I took down the paper with our first set of handprints. They'd still have the ones on the walls. I dropped the pins into the corner of the suitcase, set the paper flat on top of my clothes, and snapped the suitcase shut as Father opened the door.

"We need to go," he said. He took my suitcase and we all went downstairs to the front door. "Kammi and Tye, give Mathilde a good hug, and go out to play."

Tye hugged me as if this was any afternoon: a good, quick squeeze. Then she scampered out to find her friends.

When would she notice what it really meant that I wasn't around? When I wasn't home for dinner? When Kammi claimed my bed? When I hadn't been home for a week? Two? If she noticed more meat on the table, thicker stockings to replace the hand-me-downs with holes? Would they let these things become linked in her mind?

She wouldn't see me again until we were grown up.

If then.

And she wouldn't remember me.

But Kammi knew. She would remember. Always. She clung to me, and I held on until Father pulled us apart. Her hair was falling out of its braid from rubbing against my sweater; her face was pink, eyes wet.

"Go along with Tye, now," Father said. The sister she would get to grow up with.

She ran off without her coat, even though it was cold.

Leaving Mother, Father, and me.

. . .

We walked slowly, one parent on either side of me, a solemn parade. Other people caught my eye on the way to the train and nodded their goodbyes. But no one tagged along.

When soldiers left, people cheered and wished them good luck. Gave them kisses and sweets. Followed them to the station, waved from the platform.

Mother put her hand on my back. "Remember, it's not about you or that they think you are doing the wrong thing. They don't know what to think, so they're putting themselves first."

A lump rose in my throat. We passed my favorite bakery. When would I taste their glazed buns again? They had only plain ones in the winter, but in the summer they put raspberries in the glaze. Each bite was perfect, like heaven.

But heaven was only an idea. Nowhere was safe and peaceful for eternity.

Father followed my gaze, and ducked into the shop. He returned, beaming, handing me a small paper bag.

"Thank you." I clung to the bag as we walked.

Megs appeared before me, her dark braids tidy, her cheeks pink in the cold, her eyes bright.

Megs.

She hugged me tightly, and disappeared without a word.

Any words, all the words, must have gotten stuck in our throats.

My parents and I walked through the doors of the train station under the great clock. A few people waited on benches. I looked up at the board.

"Father." I tugged his coat. He was looking around the

station as if he'd never been there before, though he had. "There's no two-thirteen on the board."

"Hmm." He frowned.

Was this the right station? Was the train canceled?

My arms relaxed at my side. If there was no train, I would have to go back home.

Mother said, "We'll ask the stationmaster; he's at his window."

Father nodded and led the way over.

The stationmaster looked up at us. "Yes?"

"My daughter was scheduled for the two-thirteen today, but there's not one on the board."

"Ah. Your daughter's name?"

"Mathilde Joss."

He met my eyes. "You have identification?"

Father took some folded papers and a little card out of his inside breast pocket and handed them to the stationmaster, who reviewed them and then studied me.

Then he said, "Yes, I have Miss Joss scheduled on the two-thirteen, which will be arriving on track two in twenty minutes. You may wait with her there, but you will not be permitted to board the train. No exceptions."

"Of course," Mother said.

"Of course," Father echoed.

"I'd suggest that you let Miss Joss carry her own identification cards from now on, Mr. Joss." And he handed the papers back to me, not to Father.

I put them deep into my own breast pocket.

We left the window.

"Do you want to use the washroom?" Mother asked.

"No."

"Do you want to sit?" Father asked.

I looked around at the ordinary people: expecting arrivals, headed on their own travels ... all hoping to see their loved ones soon.

I couldn't sit with them. I wasn't like them. Not anymore.

"No. Let's just go up to the platform."

There wasn't anybody else on track two.

"Well, you shouldn't have any trouble finding a seat," Father joked as we walked down the platform.

The wind whistled, cold, across the raised platform.

Father handed me an envelope.

"You already gave me a treat." But I lifted the flap of the envelope anyway. "You can't give me this!"

"Of course I can. It's thanks to you we have it."

"But you need it."

"We have enough. If you ever need money, I would rather you have some. Keep it close. Here." He took the envelope, opened my coat, and tucked it into the inside pocket. Then he straightened my coat and looked around cautiously, but there still wasn't anyone there but the three of us.

"I—" I looked into Father's eyes, which were gazing back at me with warmth and calm and love; I turned to Mother, who looked sad, but just as resolute as Father. "I—"

This would to be the hardest thing I ever had to say to them.

Especially as it might also be the last thing I ever said to them.

"I want you to go."

"You can't get on the train by yourself," Mother protested.

Father studied me. "Of course she can. She'll be on the train without us, she can wait for the train without us."

Mother bit her lip. Then she nodded, but she looked hurt.

I lowered my eyes. "If I wait to say goodbye when the train gets here, we'll only have a minute, and I might not get on. If we say goodbye now . . ."

Father folded his arms around me tight. He smelled properly of the post office today, and I breathed in deeply to seal it in my memory.

*The last hug, the last hug . . .*

A lifetime and an instant later, Father let go and kissed me on the head. "Do as you're told. Be a good girl. We're so proud of you, Big."

Then Mother's thinner arms clung to me. She moved a hand from my back to my head, pressing me against her chest. I could hear her heart beating; I closed my eyes, remembering it deep within me as the first sound I'd ever heard.

"I'll be all right," I said when we broke apart.

*You'll be all right.*

"I know."

Father put his arm around her.

What was left to say?

"Work hard," Father said. "The sooner you can help end the war, the sooner you can be back with us. Things will be even better then, and you will have made them so."

I nodded.

"I do believe this is the right thing," Mother reminded me. "We'll think of you every day. We love you."

"I love you, too."

Father gave me one last smile, and set my suitcase at my feet. Then he and Mother started down the platform toward the station. Mother looked back over her shoulder as he guided her, holding my gaze for another moment, until she had to turn to go down the stairs.

Now we were going in different directions.

I was really alone.

*Mother and Father, walking back, arm in arm, together but lonely, their hearts aching already.*

*Mother weeping.*

I shook my head.

No. No, she wouldn't weep. She would hold her head up. To show the neighbors she'd made the right choice. Like she'd told me.

I sat down on my suitcase.

The station clock read 2:13 exactly when the train came to a stop.

A young woman in a navy uniform set just one foot onto the platform, her hand clinging to the bar in the doorway.

"Mathilde Joss?"

# 14

I SAT IN AN empty compartment, staring at the last views of Lykkelig as we pulled away from the station.

I'd ridden on a train twice before.

One summer, our family had gone north, to the seaside.

Another summer, Megs's father had taken just the two of us south to the mountains for a picnic day. Before he went away. Before there was no money for extra things like train fares. Before there was nothing to put in a picnic basket.

Before the war.

The train attendant came back. "I'll see your papers now."

She read them, and smiled at me as she handed them back. She took out a ticket and punched it several times.

"We should be there late tonight. I'll come by to make sure you're not asleep. There's a washroom at the end of the corridor in each car, and there's a dining car two cars back. I've punched your ticket to show you have two prepaid meals, so you can eat whatever you like."

"Thank you."

Who'd have thought joining the army would have gotten

me treated like the Queen of Eilean? Two paid-for meals on the train!

What would the food be like wherever I was going?

Chugging along through the countryside, you might not have known there was a war. Peaceful snow laced fields of chill winter green. Gray stone steeples peeked up from between the hills. Cows huddled together along fences.

But in cities, and just outside them, workers sifted through heaps of rubble with shovels. Blackened shells of aerials littered bombed aerstrips.

None of these places had names. All the signage had been painted over black.

If there was a station left to stop in, we picked up khaki-clad soldiers. Sometimes we stopped to collect them in the middle of woods or fields. How did they know to meet the train there?

The sky grew overcast, and the gray threatened to settle inside me. I decided to go for a walk and have something to eat.

I took my ticket and walked back a car. It was full of soldiers sitting on rows and rows of bench seats, some facing each other. I kept my eyes down as I walked through.

I sat at an empty table in the dining car and a waiter handed me a menu with a few choices on it. Any choice was still more than I'd ever had at home. I ordered a meat patty with gravy and beans. When every bite was gone, I scraped my fork against the plate and didn't leave a single drop of sauce.

I made my way through the soldiers' car again on the way back to my compartment.

"Hey, little sister," one of the soldiers called.

I froze.

Several soldiers were looking at me.

"Aren't many civilians traveling on this train. You lost?" the same soldier asked.

"I'm supposed to be here. I'm in the service now, too."

"Are you?" The soldier leaning forward a bit, elbows lazily on his knees. "And what do you do in the service?"

"I don't know."

"Hmm . . ." He raised his eyebrows and pursed his lips thoughtfully, rubbing his chin. "A mission so secret you don't even know what it is?"

I shrugged.

"Sending little children on top-secret missions now? How did they find you, little sister?"

"I'm nobody's little sister."

"You're everyone's little sister. What you're doing on this train is beyond me. Budge over, Henning," he said to the soldier beside him, and looked back to me. "Have a seat."

I sat—what did I have to do for the rest of the day anyway? I might as well be friendly and get used to soldiers. Maybe I was going to the same place they were.

"You play?" He shuffled a deck of cards.

"No."

The boys started to play, and I watched for a few hands. I studied the cards they put down, and when they picked up new ones. The one called Henning would scratch his nose before selecting a new card, so I knew if he liked his hand. The one next to him would sit with his feet crossed until he knew that he liked his hand, and when he relaxed, his feet uncrossed.

"You in?" the first soldier asked eventually.

I nodded.

He dealt me in, and on my first game, I won.

# 15

"MATHILDE . . . MATHILDE . . ."

A gentle hand shook my shoulder.

"We'll be arriving at your stop shortly. I've gotten your suitcase down for you. Here, put your coat on. . . ."

The train attendant held my coat behind me as if I were as young as Tye. I sleepily extended my arms to each side in turn. She pulled my braids out for me and tugged the coat closed in front of me.

The drowsiness was hard to shake off. For the first time in weeks, I'd fallen asleep without being afraid. Trains and their tracks and stations were often bombed, as I'd seen earlier, but I hadn't worried about hearing sirens, about being jolted from my sleep. The train's movement had kept me feeling safe and sleepy, and my stomach was full for the first time since I could remember. I'd had my second meal with the soldiers, and then eaten my glazed bun for dessert back in my compartment.

"Come, stand by the door. . . ."

I followed her, carrying my suitcase. Out the window,

the dark grass and trees racing by slowed and suddenly a platform appeared.

When the train stopped, the attendant opened the door, looked around, and nodded to me to exit.

"Goodbye, Mathilde."

"Goodbye."

She was already latching the door shut. As the train pulled away, I waved at the windows where the soldiers slept, cards put away and dinners eaten.

I looked up and down the dark platform.

A light flickered. I covered my face with my arm as it flashed into my eyes.

A figure walked toward me: a woman.

When she reached me, she said, "Your papers, please."

I handed over my papers with a steady hand, which she seemed to notice by the way her eyes and flashlight moved momentarily from my hand to my face, and she nodded her approval. She turned the flashlight to read my papers. Then she snapped the flashlight off and my eyes adjusted to the starlit night.

The woman started to walk down the platform and I hurried to keep up, lugging my suitcase.

"We have a bit of a carriage ride ahead of us," she said. "No car. We've got a cart and pony. But maybe—you like ponies?"

Did I like ponies?

I didn't answer. I hadn't been expecting such a question.

We came off the platform steps—no station house here—but the creature attached to the waiting cart didn't look small enough to be a pony. I stood, gaping at him, until the woman said, "Let's go, or we'll have no sleep whatsoever tonight. Put your suitcase in the back and come sit with me up front."

I hurried to do what she asked. When I plopped down beside her, she told the giant pony to go with a shake of the reins.

"I'm Miss Ibsen."

"Yes, Miss Ibsen."

We traveled on what seemed to be a dirt road through woods. The darkness, the lull of the turning wheels, and the pony's clomping made me sleepy again. But there wasn't anywhere good to lean—I would either slump sideways onto Miss Ibsen, or tumble out the open side of the cart.

I yawned.

"I know, it's awful. But we can't choose the train schedules, I'm afraid. We'll get you to bed soon enough. So, what are your interests, Mathilde?"

"What?" The question surprised me, like the one about ponies.

"I'll keep you awake by talking to you. Unless you'd prefer to curl up in the back with your suitcase?"

Was that really an option, to curl up with my suitcase? "Oh—talking is fine."

"In that case, what *are* your interests?"

What *were* my interests? Was it just my being sleepy that made my brain sluggish?

"I guess what I like best is playing with my friend Megs."

"Where do you play?"

"In the woods outside the city."

"You are from Lykkelig?"

"Yes."

"Do you have brothers and sisters?"

"Sisters," I said, a tight knot forming in my stomach. Not for thinking of them, but for having *not* thought of them until now. How had that happened?

"I grew up in a town up north, not as large as your city, but not too small, either."

"And what do you do now?" I asked. Maybe it would be a clue as to what *I* was meant to do.

"You'll find out in time." She laughed. "As far as you know, I'm some sort of midnight cart-and-pony chauffeur."

No aerials disturbed our ride. The train must have traveled northwest, deeper into Sofarende, farther from the border.

A large manor house rose up out of the gloomy darkness, surrounded by a wall at least one story high.

"Welcome to Faetre," Miss Ibsen said.


Two soldiers stood at the gate.

"Miss Ibsen," one greeted her. "Another one?"

"Another one!"

"We need more?" the other soldier teased.

"We do."

"Won't we be full to bursting?" They were like the soldiers on the train—not at all serious.

"Nonsense. There are still rooms to spare," she answered as they waved her through.

If there were still rooms to spare, then why had the Examiner been so insistent that she didn't want Megs to come?

"We don't like the security to look too tight," Miss Ibsen said. "Not from the air, anyway. There are more soldiers here than just them, don't worry."

Was that a reason not to worry? Or a reason *to* worry? Was this a known military base? A secret place?

I thought of a safer question as we pulled along the side of the impressive building: "How many rooms are there?"

"One hundred forty!"

"Really?"

"Originally, this was the summer house of a baron, and then it was a boarding school. It's ours now."

We rode to stables around the back. Another soldier handed me my suitcase as I hopped down from the cart, and took over the pony.

"Come along," Miss Ibsen said to me. I followed her to the main entryway, which she opened with three different keys. She held the door open, and I stepped inside into the pitch-dark.

Miss Ibsen followed me inside, shut the door, and re-bolted all the locks. Then she lit a match and a candle from the hallway table. "Best save my flashlight for when I'm outside."

The tiny flame illuminated a large foyer with hallways and rooms leading off in several directions, and a grand staircase. The great windows to the front of the house had been covered with black curtains.

"So aerials can't see us at night," she explained. "Though we tend to have rather quiet nights around here. It's just a precaution. This way." She led me through the largest archway off the foyer. We walked toward a large, open living room, which also had black curtains over its two-story windows, though it was brighter because of a lit electric light on a side table. The room contained clusters of comfortable chairs around both low and high tables, and all the tables were set with board games. Miss Ibsen paused in the doorway.

A head of shoulder-length light brown hair peeked over the back of one of the sofas.

I followed Miss Ibsen around to the front of the sofa.

A girl my age was sitting there.

"Annevi!" Miss Ibsen said. "What are you doing up?"

"I had an idea." She didn't look up from her board game.

"You couldn't think about it in your room?"

"I needed the board."

I stiffened. What was the punishment for being out of your room at night?

"Solve anything?" Miss Ibsen asked, warm curiosity rather than sternness in her voice.

Annevi shook her head. Disappointment and slight frustration crossed her face. But not shame or fear.

"Try again in the morning. Maybe your mind will solve it in your sleep."

Annevi nodded, though she didn't seem sleepy. She stood, but kept her eyes on the board. She reached out and moved a couple of pieces.

"Come upstairs with us. This is Mathilde."

"Hi," Annevi said, though she didn't even look at me. She didn't seem at all surprised to see a new girl showing up at nearly dawn.

"The light, Annevi."

Annevi switched off the electric light.

We proceeded upstairs, and up some more stairs to the third floor and a corridor lined with doors.

"Good night, Annevi. I'll see you at breakfast."

Annevi disappeared behind one of the doors.

"We're putting you just a few doors down, along here." Miss Ibsen opened another door on the opposite side.

I stepped into the tiny room and looked around.

I'd assumed I'd share sleeping quarters—if we slept inside at all—but there was a single, unoccupied bed; a desk; a window with its own heavy black curtain; and several bookshelves full of books.

Miss Ibsen snapped on the electric overhead light with a switch by the door. "Always make sure your curtain is pulled before putting on your lights at night."

I nodded.

"There's a washroom down the hall."

I nodded again.

"Get some rest now."

She left, shutting the door, but she didn't mention breakfast. Or seeing me in the morning. Or what to do if sirens sounded in the night.

Her footsteps faded away, and it was too late to ask; I'd wake everyone up by calling or running after her, and she'd been so careful to be quiet.

I left my door open and tiptoed to the washroom. I flipped the light switch and found three separate toilets behind their own doors, three bathing tubs behind pull curtains, and three sinks along the wall.

I went back to my room, turned out the lights, and lay down.

What kind of job was this, what kind of place, where you could get up in the middle of the night just to think about your board game and not get in trouble for being out of bed?

I stared into the darkness.

How would I ever get to sleep?

No Kammi and Tye, softly breathing, occasionally turning over.

They hadn't even given me other girls sleeping near me that I could imagine were my sisters.

The night was eerily quiet.

I got up and opened my suitcase to find my nightclothes. Instead, I lifted out the handprints painting, and hugged it to my chest.

# 16

I LAY FLAT ON my stomach in bed.

It was still dark.

And quiet.

But a different sort of dark and quiet.

A bird chirped. A child laughed.

I stood and drew back the black curtain. Bright sunlight poured in. Blinking, squinting, I took in the yard below, the green woods around the house. Beyond that rolled dark, green hills and more woods until the alternating patches sloped into steep purple-gray mountains.

For sun that bright in winter, it must have been midday. "Midday!"

I was late on my very first day!

I tried to straighten my clothes, which were rumpled from the train and then from sleeping in them. There wasn't any hope of fixing my braids, so I just smoothed the loose strands behind my ears. No one was along the hallway to ask where to go. I spent a minute in the washroom, and then thundered down the nearest stairs, and the next set after that, and raced down the main staircase toward the grand foyer.

And there was the Examiner.

I froze on the steps. What could I say to apologize for oversleeping?

But she smiled and said, "Ah. Mathilde. Welcome to Faetre. Did you have a good rest?"

"I—uh—I . . ."

"Come on, it's time for your haircut."

"My what?"

"Haircut. Come on."

Oh no! I hadn't gotten my braids in order and now they were going to chop them off!

I scurried to keep up with her as she left the foyer and headed down a hallway lined with closed doors. She pushed one open.

There was Miss Ibsen, looking refreshed and not as if she had been up driving pony carts in the night. She sat at a desk, tapping something out on a typewriter.

"Mathilde, for her haircut," the Examiner said.

"Oh!" she said, hopping up. "Mathilde! How was your sleep?"

"Good. Um . . ."

They both remained silent, waiting for me to continue.

"Why do I have to have my hair cut?"

"We feed you and wash your clothes, but we can't be chasing after all of you to brush your hair every day. Short so you can take care of it yourself. No fuss, please," the Examiner said.

Miss Ibsen set newspaper on the floor and placed a

wooden chair over it. She got sharp silver scissors and a comb from her desk and stood by the chair.

No fuss.

It was like sitting another test.

I took a deep breath and sat down.

Miss Ibsen's touch was more gentle even than Mother's as she loosened my braids and combed my hair out straight. The scissors snipped loudly. I kept my head down, watching my blond tails collect on the floor.

After a time, Miss Ibsen set aside the scissors and pulled some of the hair from the top of my head over to one side, tying it there to keep it out of my eyes. She handed me a mirror.

"I think it looks nice," she said.

My hair was cut just above my shoulders.

It didn't look as blond with the ends cut off.

With the tails went the sun-bleached hours of summer.

A lump rose in my throat as I looked away from the mirror and down at the hair on the floor.

"Come, Mathilde," the Examiner said, but she spoke more kindly than she had before.

I forced a weak smile at Miss Ibsen, who was smiling at me, and I scooted to keep up with the Examiner.

Maybe I was finally going to find out what this was all about. What the test had been for and why I'd come all this way. And had my hair chopped. My new job.

"You will rise and dress by eight every morning," said the Examiner. "Eight to eight-thirty, there's a brisk walk around the grounds; eighty-thirty, breakfast. Lunch at noon. Two to three is playtime outside, that's mandatory, and very important. We need to keep this place looking like a school, and exercise keeps your mind sharp. Dinner at six, in your room by ten, lights out is up to you, though keep those curtains pulled. We expect you to rest well each night so that you are fresh for your daytime activities."

Like playtime? Had we come here just to disguise this place as a school?

I was almost running to keep up as she continued along the hallway, but then she turned into the enormous living room.

It was full of kids.

Playing board games.

Shouting, laughing, arguing.

Moving pieces, setting them up a different way, going back to the way they were before. Walking between the boards to move pieces to other boards. Changing the moves other people had just made.

Answering telephones at stations along the walls. Calling out to others around a board game, who would move the pieces, argue some more.

Despite the noise, the room had an intensity of deep concentration.

Some people were quiet. Reading, studying maps.

A few adults walked around the room, observing, asking questions.

But not giving direction or orders. They weren't interfering at all.

"What do you want me to do?" I asked.

"Observe. Try things out. See what interests you. You may also read anything you see here or in your room. Lunch will be served shortly. You must be hungry."

I was. Though I'd been so distracted I hadn't noticed until she mentioned it.

Then she left me.

Okay.

I'd been instructed to observe. But not to stand frozen like a statue in the middle of the entryway.

I tiptoed in.

I spotted Annevi, sitting alone on her couch, staring at her board game, just as she had been last night. Her hair was cut like mine, I realized. She even had the same lock of hair pulled away from her eyes. So did all the other girls in the room.

How had these girls looked before? Had they had long hair like mine? Had it felt strange to them, too, to have it cut?

I ran my hand through mine, my fingers tingling as they met the fresh edges.

Annevi also ran her hands through her hair, gripping it near her scalp from time to time, but she wasn't thinking about her hair. Just about her game.

I took the chair across from her.

"Hi, Mathilde." She hadn't looked up.

"Hi."

I studied the board, too.

It wasn't a game. It was a grid with a faint sort of map underneath. Little red ships sat on top.

"So what are you good at?" Annevi asked, not taking her eyes off the board.

"Me?"

"Yes, you."

"Nothing."

She looked up then, her green-brown eyes meeting mine.

"You have to be good at something." She looked back down and slid one of the red ships over two places, paused, and slid it back. "Otherwise you wouldn't be here."

"I'm not."

She looked up again, a bit bewildered, as if I was playing stupid. Her gaze moved from me to a girl absorbed in a fat book of military history. "Fredericka can remember anything she reads. *Anything*." Her gaze moved to a tall boy who seemed to be giving out directions at two or three board tables at once. "Tommy, he can hold multiple formations in his head at once and see the patterns they share." She nodded toward a shorter, slightly chubby boy on a telephone. "Hamlin. Expert at languages. Fluent in seven, could learn a new one between now and dinnertime. He can take any incoming message and translate it, even in code."

"He—"

"See her over there, the napping girl?"

"Yes, she—"

"Not napping. Deciphering. Reads the messages, a whole bunch of them, closes her eyes, sometimes for hours, but when she opens them—messages clear. Get it?"

"I—" I felt cold all the way through my stomach.

There *must* have been a mistake. I couldn't even picture Megs fitting in here. These kids were all super-geniuses.

"What are . . ."

But Annevi was staring at the board again. I stared, too. What did she see? Or rather, it seemed that she *wasn't* seeing something.

What could *I* see?

Nothing but little red ships. Sometimes a shape stood out, a triangle here or there.

But I didn't even know what I was supposed to see.

"Are there . . . ships all traveling together in this formation?"

"No, no . . . it's just three ships . . . shown over time." Annevi rocked back and forth slightly. Her fingers gripped her hair tight along her scalp. Then she was still again.

We both went back to staring.

After several minutes, Annevi swept all the pieces off the board in one movement, sending them flying across the room.

I blinked and sat back. I looked around, but nobody else had reacted.

Annevi plopped back down and stared at the blank board.

Then she stood up, triumphant relief on her face, and shouted, "Tommy! Call downstairs! Check three-D! All of them in three-D!"

"Excellent, Annevi, excellent!" Tommy grabbed the nearest telephone, dialed, and said into it, "Annevi thinks she's got them, check three-D. Okay. Okay." He hung up and called to Annevi, "We should know in eight hours."

She nodded and sank back onto her sofa, breathing as if she'd just run several miles.

One of the adults came over. "Well done, Annevi."

"Can I have the next one?"

"Collect your ships from the floor, and then rest until lunch. Why don't you show Mathilde the art room?"

Annevi crawled around, not paying any attention to where other people were stepping as she found her ships. I grabbed the ones near me and handed them to her when she came back.

"Come on," Annevi said to me in a resigned sort of way. Once we were in the hallway, she said, "The proctors are big on 'recreation' around here. They seem to think it's healthy to visit the art room. You can go there whenever you like, no one would stop you if you said you needed to go to the art room."

She made it sound like going to the washroom. A necessity, and so private your decision to go there wasn't to be questioned.

Annevi led me down a dark hallway away from where I'd gotten my hair cut, toward the other side of the house. She opened the door to a room with large windows, several tables, a paint-spattered sink, and shelves and shelves of art supplies. More than I'd ever seen.

"Go ahead, you can use anything you like."

I took familiar things—white paper, paintbrushes, and watercolors—and filled a small jar with water from the sink. I sat at a table and started to paint back the summer: smooth green hills, bright trees . . .

Annevi took a bunch of blank newspaper and balled it up; then she mixed thick blue and white paint to make baby blue, and brushed it sloppily all over the newspaper ball.

I was staring at this mess when one of the proctors came in.

"Lovely, girls, what are you making?"

"The world," Annevi said. "The world is mostly water, so it probably looks blue from far away."

"That's insightful, Annevi. Mathilde, have you drawn where you're from?"

"Sort of." I shook my head, still unused to the lightness of shorter, freer hair.

"It's lunchtime," the woman said.

Annevi disappeared at once.

The proctor continued to look at me kindly, and seemed quite interested in my painting. "Is it finished?"

"I think so," I said.

"Wonderful! There we go!" She pinned my painting to the otherwise bare wall of the art room.

"Why haven't you hung up anyone else's artwork?"

"Theirs tends not to be . . . flat." She looked over at Annevi's abandoned world.

*Flat* would not have been a good word in the art room back at school. Flat things lacked depth. Did she think my picture was boring? It was just a landscape, not even a real place.

But she'd hung it up and was studying it as if it was very interesting.

I looked at it more closely.

In the center of the trees was a gap. A gap where two girls belonged. Two girls, holding hands, one leading the other.

"Are you all right?" the woman asked me.

"Just hungry, I guess."

Lunch was in a large dining hall with long tables. Each place was set with a sandwich on a plate and a glass of milk. Kids elbowed and bumped into each other as friends looked for seats together and swapped plates for reasons I couldn't understand yet.

I sat in front of an untouched plate and realized I hadn't eaten since the train, which seemed like a time from another life. The sandwich was chopped egg; I devoured it and gulped down the milk.

The girl across from me stared at me as I wiped my mouth on my sleeve.

"Don't worry," said the girl next to me. "We were all hungry when we got here. But you'll get plenty now, it's not like back home. I'm Caelyn."

"Mathilde."

"I'm Brid," said the girl across from me.

"So . . . what happens here?" I asked.

"Just what you see happen," Caelyn said carefully.

"Annevi solved some kind of puzzle and they called the answer downstairs."

"Oh, did she solve it?" Caelyn asked. "She's been on that one all week, no one could figure out *what* had become of those dybnauts, they weren't showing up on any scans."

"Dybnauts?"

"Deep, undersea boats."

"Tommy said they'd know in eight hours."

"She rarely misses," Caelyn said. "She's probably right."

I peered down the table at Annevi, who had taken her sandwich apart and was eating it from the inside out, laughing as she talked with some boys.

"What's . . . downstairs?"

"Grown-ups," Brid said. "They get the incoming calls and place the outgoing ones, and they have the . . . you know."

I shook my head.

Brid and Caelyn looked at each other, and then back at me. "Big decoding machines," Caelyn whispered. "Downstairs is also where we go if bombers fly over. It's under three layers of concrete and steel."

"Do we go down there a lot?"

"Never," Caelyn said, neatly biting her sandwich. "But I've heard there's enough food stored for us all to live on for three years."

"Three years?"

"Yeah. So if Tyssia comes we can stay here, pretending to be a school, and keep doing our work. Bring them down from the inside."

My sandwich must have gotten stuck in my throat. I wished I had more milk.

"What have they asked you to do?" Brid asked.

"Nothing, yet."

"Stick with Tommy," Caelyn said. "You can learn a lot from him. He can do everything, and all at once."

Tommy had been the center of a huge flurry of activity. Not really where I wanted to be.

When we went back upstairs, an extremely anxious Annevi was soothed with coordinates of new ships to set up. I sat across from her and watched her slide ships into their formations. Maybe if I saw the puzzle from the beginning I could solve it. But I didn't understand this one any better than the last.

I followed Annevi and the others outside at playtime. Annevi marched over to a crowd huddled around one boy with a bag. The kids were all twisting away to reach blindly into the cloth sack, pulling out strips of fabric. Most of them exclaimed or groaned when they saw the colors of their bands, but started tying them around their arms.

The bands were either twisted black and orange, or white and aqua blue.

"What is this?" I asked Annevi, who was now tying a white and blue band around my arm.

"Tyssia Tag. Those other armbands used to be black. Caelyn made us new ones with orange after Tyssia joined with Erobern."

And the blue and white was of our own, seafaring country.

"You have to get the other country's armbands. The country who gets all the other armbands wins."

"They make you play war games at playtime?"

"Make us?" Annevi looked mystified. "No! *We* made this up! Run, go!"

I ran.

We could run anywhere we wanted, as long as we stayed within the walls, but there was plenty of space and trees.

Running felt good, despite the cold; my heart and lungs worked to keep up with my feet. As I grew warmer and felt the air on my face and legs, summer wasn't that far away, summer when Megs and I had run in the woods like this. I ran so fast no one claimed my armband, and I forgot about it.

I'd come to fight in the war; I was far from home and the people I loved. But it was so different from the war I knew: aerials and bombing, empty stomachs. The anxiety of what could happen at any time. Instead of being brought closer to the war, it seemed I had been brought farther away.

• • •

After playtime, I pinned up my sisters' handprints in my room.

The hardest thing about the distance from the war was not being able to tell Mother and Father that I was safe. Would they worry constantly? Or would they choose to believe that I was all right?

They probably would believe I was safe. That had been the whole point of sending me.

And, so far, it seemed true.

A pit formed in my stomach. Why should I be safe when the people I loved couldn't be?

And I wasn't anything like these kids. I wasn't smart like they were. I didn't really belong.

Megs had said there had to be something only I could do. She was usually right. So if she thought there was something I could do, maybe there was.

Father had said to help bring the war to an end, and then I could go home.

I wanted him to be proud of me.

I'd take Caelyn's advice: stick with Tommy and see if I couldn't be useful at *something*.

# 17

"HANS, WHAT'S IN BLOCK THREE-E?"

"Three-B?"

"E! Three-elephant!"

"Oh! Nothing!"

"Nothing?"

"It's empty. E for empty."

"There should be something there, should be something..." Tommy paced between four boards, where a dozen kids sat, considering possibilities, moving pieces.

He slammed into me.

For the fifth time.

The first four times, he had stepped to the side and ignored me. I kept opening my mouth to say something, but nothing came out. The last time, he stared into my face as if only then seeing me.

"Who are you?"

"Mathilde."

"Can I help you?"

"I—I'm trying to figure out what to do."

"Aren't we all? Here." He shoved a clipboard at me. The papers on it were incredibly crumpled from being flipped through so many times. "If anyone at these tables moves anything, mark the change on the paper, okay?"

"Okay."

A page represented each table with a chart numbered to match the squares on the board. I stood at each table and confirmed that the Xs matched the pieces' placements. But as soon as the kids started moving the pieces, I couldn't keep up. I turned from one table to another, then back, and those first kids would have moved something again.

The clipboard was wrenched out of my hands.

I jumped.

Tommy studied my notes. "There is such order in it, and yet, it's not without mystery."

"What isn't?"

"This. These plots. Math. Maybe I should make an equation showing the typical movements."

But he was speaking to himself; he scribbled down some notes and thrust the clipboard back. "Keep up."

I tried my best.

"Lykkelig."

Someone had said the name of my city. I looked around.

I was supposed to be the only one chosen from there, so why would anyone be talking about it? Was someone talking about me?

I missed several more changes as I looked to see who had spoken.

And then they said it again—three boys on couches at a low table across the room.

As I got closer, I could hear that they were arguing about a lot of cities.

"No, that town got hit three nights in a row! They're going to go somewhere else now! It's too likely we have aerials ready for them! We've got to look for a new target."

"But they just hit somewhere new last night; they've never introduced new sites so close together! If not there again, then somewhere else they've already hit."

A third boy shouted, "I've been telling you, they've been accelerating the introduction of new towns!"

"All with—"

"Factories!"

"We don't have factories," I said.

"What?"

The boys looked up at me, surprised.

"We don't have factories."

"Of course we don't have factories. Faetre's just a manor house in the middle of nowhere."

"I mean we, back home. In Lykkelig."

One of the boys looked at me critically. He pulled out a book and flipped through it until he found a certain page and showed me the heading and the data below it.

"Fourteen," he said. "Fourteen factories."

Tommy yanked the clipboard out of my hands again, and ran back over to his tables.

I sat down. "I didn't know that. Is that why they've been bombing?"

"Factories. Train stations. Morale," one of the boys said, like he was reciting a school lesson. His tone made me assume his list was in order of importance.

The board before them—a map of Sofarende—was marked with a smattering of colored pegs.

"All the bombings from the past week. We've got to predict tonight's. We send our predictions downstairs by dinner."

"And what do they do with them?"

"Pass them along to the Aerial Department, if they want to."

"Do you hear how often you're right?"

"Every morning we get the information about who's been bombed last night. Then we know."

"How often are you right?"

"More often than not."

I studied the pegs.

One of the boys followed my eyes, and explained, "Blue for last night, yellow for the night before that, red before that, green before that, black, then white . . . tomorrow we'll shift the white ones to represent tonight's, as last night's."

He rattled this off and my head spun, trying to sort it out.

"Where's the board with overall bombings?"

Another boy smiled. He knew I was catching on.

"The next table. All red pins. Represents the number of times for each city."

I glanced over. Lykkelig was completely covered with red pegs.

They started arguing again. Tossing out the names of towns coldly, compared to the flames licking at my heart. My hands tightened into fists. The sixth time that they mentioned Lykkelig that way, I yelled, "Haven't your towns been bombed? Doesn't it mean anything to you, to sit here and discuss which towns are next? What happens if you make a mistake?"

They stared at me. So did several of the children nearby.

One of the boys said, "We have to be objective."

Another said, "That's how we'll help them!"

And the third, the one who had smiled at me earlier, said, "Of course it does."

His companions stared at him.

"We aren't there anymore," the first boy said as he turned back to the board. "We're safe here."

"But aren't your families still there?"

"Who knows."

The third boy pointed to a town marked with two colored pegs. "My family's there. Or they were when I left. *I* worry about them."

He held my eyes. I felt a little better.

"We have half an hour left to decide, and if we don't, we won't be helping anyone." The second boy glanced at the clock.

"I'll let you get on with it, then," I said. The Examiner had entered the room; she was watching me. Having failed at helping Tommy, I didn't want to be seen ruining this task, too. I started to get up.

"Wait," the third boy said. "I'm Gunnar."

"Mathilde." I sat back down.

I stayed with them until their call downstairs, though I kept quiet, even when they came to the conclusion that we should expect another air raid over Lykkelig that night.

· · ·

After a dinner of chicken soup and bread, I was so tired, but desperately wanted to take a bath. To wash off the train's smoke and the itchy feel of the haircut from my neck.

The guilt that I would be safe tonight, and my family would not. Could you rinse away guilt?

Miss Ibsen showed me where to find the towels, and handed me a new bar of soap and a comb that were to be my own.

"Do you have a bathrobe?" she asked. I shook my head. She found me a new navy boy's robe and wrote *MJ* on the inner label with a marking pen. "You can wear it to and from your room."

I nodded.

After I'd changed, I set my towel on the stool next to a tub and worked out the taps and the drain plug. While I waited for the tub to fill, the door opened and Annevi came in, wearing a robe and carrying her soap. She got a towel and turned on the water in the next tub.

"Did they send you, too?" she asked.

"Send me? No."

"They'll send you to take a bath every couple days."

"Oh."

I turned off my taps, pulled the curtain around my bathtub, and got into the tub. I went under to wet my head, and then I just sat. Annevi turned off her taps and pulled her curtain.

One of my taps dripped: *Splink. Splink. Splink.*

"Did you find your new set of ships?" I asked.

"No."

*Splink. Splink. Splink.*

"They're . . . dybnauts?"

"Sometimes."

"Whose are they?"

"Ours. Or Eilean's. Or Tyssia's."

*Splink. Splink. Splink.*

I sat up straighter. "Tyssia doesn't have access to the sea."

"Of *course* they do."

"But I thought—"

"Just because something's *not* in the newspaper doesn't mean it's *not* happening."

"But—Tyssia is landlocked—how?"

"Some of the southern states must have secretly given them port access. They're out there."

I went still. Tyssia had sea access? Could they reach our ports?

Water swished in Annevi's tub.

"What happens to the ships you find?"

"Well, if they're ours, and they're still okay, we'll tell them where to go. If they're Tyssia's: ker-POW!"

A death both fiery and watery. Screaming in pain only to get a lungful of water.

"Does that . . . bother you?"

"It's a war. That's what happens."

The bombed streets at home. The people wandering, looking for their families. That *was* what happened. The Tyssians made it happen.

I remembered my soap and tried to wash my hair.

Annevi pulled the plug of her tub. She toweled off and pulled back her curtain.

I ducked underwater to rinse. When I sat up, Annevi was standing outside my tub.

She said, very quietly, "They don't tell me whether I'm looking for ours or theirs. I *have* to find them. Do you see?"

"I do. Good night, Annevi."

"Good night."

After she left, I sat, hair dripping into the cooling water.

I had come farther away from the fighting. But being here would require a different sort of fight, a different sort of bravery.

# 18

AT MORNING WORK THE next day, I decided to stick with Brid and Caelyn. Annevi didn't need or want help finding her ships. And I did *not* want to sit with the bombing-predicting boys and their cold calculations.

But as I walked in, Gunnar caught my eye. He shook his head ever so slightly.

They *hadn't* bombed Lykkelig!

I let out a breath I hadn't realized I'd been holding.

Everyone was safe for another day.

"Thank you," I mouthed.

He nodded.

But—had *his* home been bombed?

I didn't want to go ask in front of the other boys. They might make fun of him for worrying. It would have to wait.

Because they had predicted Lykkelig, did that mean somewhere else went unprotected? Did Tyssia manipulate our predictions on purpose, create a pattern and then break it?

Of course they did. The boys would have to learn to be three steps ahead of them.

I climbed up onto one of the high chairs at the table Brid and Caelyn had picked. They both had stacks of papers with gibberish printed on them.

Brid split her stack and passed me half of it.

"Look through for things that repeat, and circle them. You can use different colors for each different repeating set."

I took up the red pencil she slid across to me, and scanned the rows and rows of letters. At first I didn't see anything repeat. I wasn't even sure if it would be repeats of three letters or five or whole strings of them.

After a few minutes I looked up to see the girls circling things with quick drops of their pencils to switch colors; Caelyn held two pencils in her right hand so that she had to switch less often. They flipped through their pages pretty quickly, though sometimes they would turn back to earlier pages to note a couple more things.

"Um . . . can you read that?" I asked.

"Read it?" Caelyn asked, sounding puzzled. "We don't need to read it."

"They read it downstairs," Brid explained. "It's coded. Ciphered, actually. We look for patterns and repeats. Downstairs, they can use those to guess at common possible words, phrases, or place-names, and then line up all the letters and changes to see if they're consistent. It saves them time if we look at the pages first."

"Oh." I continued scanning my paper, whispering the letters out loud because I thought it might be easier for me to hear than see a repeat. I heard myself say "TXR" a few times, so I circled it everywhere I saw it. Maybe those letters stood in for a common word in Tyssian.

I found a couple other things. Before I knew it, we were being called for lunch. Brid took my pages back, and looked over them, circling other things here and there. "This isn't too bad."

Which meant it wasn't too good, either.

Didn't they care that they didn't know what these messages *meant*?

Outside, Annevi turned Tyssia Tag to Tyssia Tackle and managed to bring Tommy—the tallest—down to take in a faceful of moss as she stripped off his armband. My heart was already pounding from running; I didn't want to land face-first in moss.

I noticed Fredericka, the reader, sitting by herself on a low stone wall by the house.

I sat down next to her. "You don't like to play?"

"Not really. But they make everyone go outside."

"Yeah, they told me."

"Don't you like it? It looked like you were having fun."

"I was, but . . . I'm tired now." I took off my tiger-striped armband.

She nodded.

"Have you been here a long time?"

"Six months."

"Who's been here the longest?"

"Tommy. And then Hamlin."

"You're good at reading?"

"Yes," she said, though not in a conceited way.

Everyone here was good at something.

Everyone except me.

"Why did they pick us? Kids, I mean."

She shrugged. "If people are good at something, does it matter how old they are?"

I shook my head. "I guess I didn't mean like that. I guess what I meant is that I'm surprised the grown-ups saw it that way."

"I told you Tommy was the first—his dad's a mathematician at a university. Tommy used to go in as a little boy, solve puzzles and things at his father's desk, just to pass the time. Mr. Olivier, who's here downstairs, had been at the university, too, and he remembered Tommy. He thought a lot of the intelligence would seem like puzzles to Tommy. So they gave him some problems, and he thought of them in a different way than anyone else had. Then they brought him here, and looked for other kids like him."

"Tommy's father was okay with that?"

"It sounds like he was glad. It's so much safer here."

"What about your father?"

"A grocer. When there's not a lot of food, it's hard for him to make enough money for us. We always had something to eat, but he worried about how to pay for everything else. When the test came to our town, it seemed like a good idea for me to sit it. It's helped them, the money I've earned."

"Do you know what's happened to your family?"

She shook her head.

"Is it hard not to write home?"

She nodded. "They were going to—at least, I think they were going to—save up the money so that they could move somewhere safer, up north, farther from the border. If they do, I won't even know where they are."

Fredericka sounded so sad, I couldn't help putting my hand on hers. Our hands were cold.

I looked away so she could feel like she had some privacy.

The Examiner was staring at me.

Again.

Because I wasn't running and playing?

I couldn't even play right.

The bell rang for the end of playtime. The Examiner rounded everyone up to march back inside and checked all the fresh scrapes and bruises.

As I walked closer, I realized that the Examiner wasn't upset about the scrapes and bruises; she seemed to be admiring them.

Dinner was a potato-and-meat pie with a flaky crust. It was warm, delicious, and filling, though the gravy seemed to stick in my throat.

After dinner, I went to the art room.

I ran my fingers over the crayons, flipped through the stacks of colored paper. If only I could have packed a box to send to Kammi and Tye.

I got a large sheet of paper and a pencil, and sketched without thinking about what I was drawing. After a long while, I got some watercolors, mostly beiges and browns, only hints of color. I worked slowly, letting the layers dry.

The door opened and Miss Ibsen came in.

"It's time to head up to bed."

"Yes, Miss Ibsen." I started to clean up the paints and water.

She looked at my painting.

Four people sat around a table: a man, a woman, two children. They didn't have features, really. In front of each person was a heaping plate of food. A disgusting amount of food.

"Is it your family?" she asked.

I shrugged.

"The empty chair ... that would have been ... your chair?"

I rinsed my brushes out carefully.

Miss Ibsen got some pins and hung up my picture.

She put her arm around me at the door.

# 19

"WE'LL LOSE A DAY'S WORK!"

"The point precisely," the Examiner said. "You're forgetting to be children. You'll go out for the day and have fun." She beamed at everyone.

I looked to Gunnar, who shrugged. We would have to wait to know who'd been hit in last night's bombings.

We got our coats and the Examiner counted us off, five kids to one proctor. I was glad to be with Caelyn and Miss Ibsen.

"Stay with your groups," the Examiner said. "We wouldn't want to lose anyone."

"Because we know too much," Caelyn whispered.

She nodded at me as the Examiner continued, "Don't speak to anyone along the way or in the village."

The Examiner watched us as we left through the south gates. Didn't she want to go on the outing? What would she do instead?

The ground became soft as we plodded toward the village at the bottom of the hill. The stream was quick and swollen from snow melting above us on the mountain.

Annevi ran by, coat flying behind her, giving people a thwack here and there. "Tag!"

"What if she gets lost?" I asked Miss Ibsen.

"Hooting as she does? We couldn't lose Annevi if we tried," Miss Ibsen said. But she didn't sound mean. She sounded as if Annevi was a delight to her.

I wasn't loud. I could easily be lost.

"You'll be all right, too," Miss Ibsen said. "Go and be with Caelyn."

I caught up with Caelyn. We walked silently for a while. Then I asked, "Where do you come from, Caelyn?"

"Up north, by the sea."

"Do you miss your parents?"

"Yes," she said, but it didn't sound like an I'm-finished kind of yes. Her breath caught a little, as if she had been about to say more. I waited. "But not because I came here."

"What do you mean?"

"I missed them before. They died a few years ago. Them and my brothers."

"Oh no, Caelyn, I'm sorry."

She shrugged.

"What happened?"

"A flu. I had it, too, but I got better. I lived with my grandparents after that. When they heard about the test, they wanted me to be able to go to university, which they couldn't give me. They wanted me to be with other children, which they couldn't give me. At least, that's what they said."

Her voice was heavy, as if she didn't believe these things were worth being sent away for. Or as if there may have been other reasons. I thought of my picture from the night before, of the family like mine with all that food and the empty chair.

We walked in silence for a few minutes.

"Caelyn?"

"Yeah?"

"It wasn't because they didn't want you."

Caelyn linked her arm through mine and we stayed that way for the rest of the walk.

The village had a fountain in the middle, and shops. The fountain was dry, but everyone raced around it, feet slapping the cobblestones, a thunderous version of Kammi running ahead to school. Our journey to the village had taken so long that it was lunchtime. Miss Ibsen bought fifty buns at the baker's and handed them out.

After lunch, we went to the cinema!

I'd never been before.

First they played a newsreel about Sofarender and Eilean forces defending our cities.

"They're a little behind the times," the boy next to me whispered.

Our forces were still fighting, of course, but the cities and areas they were talking about hadn't been attacked in weeks. Tyssia had moved on to other cities.

One of the proctors shushed the boy.

To any strangers in the theater, it would have sounded like an ordinary "shush," but it really meant: *Top-secret. Remember, you know nothing.*

Then came the feature. A cartoon!

I knew the story. I'm sure everyone did.

A princess lived high on a hill, as we did.

She was locked in, as we were.

Away from her family, as we were.

She was rescued.

Like none of us would be.

After the cinema, we got to explore the shops. We all liked the stationer's best. In addition to pens and paper, it had gifts and toys.

While everyone else looked at the toys, I wandered over to the crisp new envelopes. I picked one up and smelled it, breathing in deeply, closing my eyes.

It smelled like him. Like Father.

My fingers itched over the sample pens. I could get a picture postcard and borrow a pen for just a minute. The stationer would surely have stamps, too.

Where was Miss Ibsen?

There, by the door, discussing the model aerials with Hamlin and a few other boys. The boys were probably complaining about structural inaccuracies in the models. And begging to bring a few back with us.

I had the money Father had given me. Buying a postcard and stamp would be no problem. I looked at the pictures, all of this village or the mountain. I bit my lip.

Not writing home was a stupid rule. And they hadn't reminded us today. How bad would it be if someone could trace my location to this village, half a day's walk from Faetre?

I grabbed a postcard, turned it over, and uncapped a pen.

I paused.

What would I say, anyway?

*Happy and safe ~ Mathilde.*

I pictured my paintings again.

Maybe just . . . *Safe . . . Mathilde.*

Why couldn't I think of what to say to them? What would they say to me?

Was this one of those things that Mother had talked about, that the Examiner had talked about? How we protected each other?

That it was easier just to say *That was the right choice* and march forward, without each other?

"Certainly are a lot of you kids here today!"

I jumped.

A man reached over me, paying for a newspaper at the counter. The headline said BORDER REMAINS STRONG. Another thing said just for self-preservation?

"Where are all you kids from?"

I knew I wasn't supposed to answer him. But wouldn't it be worse not to?

"A school," I said.

"Ah. The school up the hill. What do you study?"

"Math . . . and reading."

"Very good."

Miss Ibsen appeared at my side. She nodded to the man, ending the conversation. Then she took the pen from my hand and capped it.

# 20

IN THE MORNING, when all the kids were receiving their updates and tasks, I headed over to Gunnar.

"Lykkelig's okay," he said. "Holtzberg got hit."

His town. His home.

"I'm sorry," I said, trying to hide my relief that my family and Megs were okay for another day.

The Examiner appeared beside us.

"Gunnar," she said, "it might interest you to know that only the northwest area of Holtzberg got hit?"

Gunnar flushed pink, trying not to look too relieved in front of the other boys. He nodded his thanks, and turned to the map with the others.

"Mathilde?" the Examiner said. "Come to my office."

I hurried to follow.

"Shut the door," she said once we were inside.

I did and, in response to her nod, took the chair in front of her desk. I waited, heart thudding.

She'd heard about me talking to the man at the shop. Or trying to write home.

After a moment's silence, she said, "We've acquired a prisoner of war."

"What?"

"We're holding a Tyssian soldier."

She studied me until I couldn't wait anymore.

"Why are you telling me?"

"I'm giving you an assignment."

I stared at her.

"Part of your daily work will now include talking to him."

"You want me to . . . *talk* to him?"

The other children all had tasks that were puzzles.

She nodded.

"Haven't you already questioned him?"

"I want *you* to."

"Every day?"

"There are things you can't learn in one day."

I nodded slowly. "What do you want me to learn?"

She continued as if I hadn't asked the question. "You will talk to him alone, but you will be perfectly safe. I will check in with you every day."

"Okay." I still didn't know what I was meant to learn, but I knew I couldn't ask her again. She would have answered my question if she'd wanted to.

"You'll start this morning. Ready?"

I stared at the Examiner as she started to get up. I didn't move.

"Now?"

"Yes, now."

"Does he speak Sofarender?"

"He should. If that's not working, your Eilian is better than your Tyssian, according to the translations on your test, so try that next."

"What—" I searched for a way to rephrase my questions. "What do you want me to ask him about?"

"Nothing in particular. Just talk."

"Just . . . talk?"

"Just talk."

Just talk.

And report what I'd learned.

"What am I supposed to say to him?"

"Anything you like except about our work here."

She wasn't giving me a goal. How could I possibly succeed?

"Ready?" she asked again.

I nodded.

I wasn't allowed to say no.


She led me to an upstairs corridor of offices. Grown-ups glanced at me through their open doors as I passed; none looked twice, so I figured they weren't bothered to see me in their hallway. They were all dressed like the Examiner and doing what seemed to be paperwork. They were very quiet.

So adults worked downstairs *and* upstairs.

A lot of different things went on in this building.

Each thing secret from the others?

The Examiner paused at a door. She unlocked it and handed me a key.

"Your key will work on either side of this door. I'm going to lock you in."

Locked in.

Alone with a Tyssian soldier.

I shivered.

*Be brave, be brave.*

I wouldn't really be locked in. I'd have the key.

I took a deep breath, accepted the key, and stepped into the room.

I stood in a narrow passage along the side of the room. A metal fence went from ceiling to floor; beyond that was a second metal fence, also from ceiling to floor, so there would always be at least three feet of space between us.

On the other side of the fencing was another door. It had no doorknob. A metal plate extended from the door to cover what would have been the gap between the wall and the door.

There was a cot with blankets; a pitcher with water and a basin; an empty plate, presumably from breakfast; and a bucket with a lid.

And there he was, sitting, knees drawn to his chest.

My enemy had been aerials in the sky.

Bombs.

Hunger.

Loved ones taken away.

I had never pictured a Tyssian before.

He wasn't even old. Only a few years older than Tommy, maybe eighteen. He wore drab beige clothes. His hair was blond, like mine.

He looked up as I entered and I saw his eyes were blue, like mine.

If I had bothered to picture a Tyssian, I wouldn't have pictured him to be so much like me. My skin itched, and something heavy settled in my stomach.

He turned even paler as he stared at me. Like maybe I was a ghost.

What could I say to him?

I walked over to the fence.

Was it rude to stare when it was the enemy, when he was in a cage?

Father took me and Kammi to the zoo once.

There had been a tiger.

We couldn't get enough of looking at the tiger.

This tiger stared back at me, still waiting.

How was I supposed to begin this conversation that was to happen every day?

Standing up taller than him didn't seem to be right, so I backed up to my wall and slid down, sitting with crossed legs.

I looked at him, and started the only way I knew how:

"I'm Mathilde."

# 21

HAD HE UNDERSTOOD ME? Even if he had, me telling him my name and sitting down as if to stay awhile seemed to puzzle him.

Finally, he said, in Tyssian, "You have a message for me?"

"No."

We continued to stare at each other.

"What's your name?" I asked in Sofarender.

He paused and thought a moment; then he said, "Rainer."

We sat.

I would report that on my first day I learned his name and that was it?

They probably already knew his name. It would have been on his tags, if he still had them.

I sighed and put my head on my knees.

"You have come just to stare at me?"

"No."

"They think that I can get out of here and they have sent a tiny guard to watch me?"

"I'm not a guard."

"Then what?"

"I just came to talk to you."

He stared at me for a moment before saying "Have fun" in Tyssian, and turned to look at the wall.

As he turned, I could see that the front and back of his beige coverall was marked with big, red, fabric Xs.

Rainer was a target.

"You're quiet," Brid said to me at lunch.

"Where were you?" Caelyn asked.

The full truth caught in my throat. I hadn't been told *not* to tell the others. Maybe it was because I didn't know how they would feel about a Tyssian soldier living upstairs.

How did *I* feel about it?

"I had an assignment."

That satisfied them both. They were used to secret assignments, and not asking too many questions. To not knowing any more than they needed to.

I went to the art room, but it wasn't empty. "Oh! Hi, Tommy."

He looked up from his project.

In the time since we'd been back from our outing, he'd managed to fashion his own model aerial. He seemed to be trying to create a propeller.

"That looks good," I said. "Will it fly?"

"It coasts fine. But I thought if I could get a propeller to turn, maybe it would stay up longer. Maybe I can get propellers on both wings."

I didn't want to bother him, so I got my own art supplies and picked another table.

Tommy was never on his own for long. Soon Annevi was there, and Hamlin, and Gunnar. Annevi and Hamlin sat with Tommy, Hamlin spouting facts about how big the propellers should be based on the size of the aerial.

But Gunnar took the seat across from me.

"We think it'll be Lykkelig tonight."

I looked over at the wall, where my feasting family hung.

My stomach squirmed.

"Oh," I managed to say.

Gunnar had followed my eyes to the painting.

"And Holtzberg again?" I asked.

"They got a lot of factories last night. We don't think they'll repeat. Maybe, but we recommended sending the defenses to other towns."

Did the Examiner recruit especially in cities that were being bombed? Were targeted places just more populated? Or were the parents more willing to send their children away?

"I'm sorry," I said. "But I'm glad it sounded like your family was okay last night."

The pencil shook in my hand and eventually I lowered it to rest on the table.

"How do you not just tell them to send the defenses to your own town, every night?"

Gunnar slid the paper I'd gotten over to his side of the table. He gently took the pencil from my hand. He sketched. A rectangle, set in a row of others: a building, on a block. Smaller rectangles: windows. Circles: faces, in the windows.

His home? His family?

Could have been any home, any family.

He looked back up at me.

"Because other people matter, too."

# 22

IN THE MORNING, I let myself into Rainer's room.

He looked up.

"You're back," he said in Sofarender, sounding surprised.

"I'll come back every day." I sat down.

After a few minutes, he said, "You do not have school? Sofarenders do not go to school?"

"We go to school." I couldn't say why *I* didn't go to school, because I couldn't explain where we were.

He looked at me suspiciously.

"It is morning-time," he said, nodding up toward the small window high in the wall that let him see the sky. No black curtain. He didn't have a candle or flashlight, so he couldn't make any light that would need to be blacked out. He spent every night in the dark. Hours and hours of it.

"Morning-time is when little children go to school, no?"

I shrugged.

He thought I was just a little child.

We were done talking.

. . .

Lunch seemed oddly quiet. I looked around. "Where's Tommy?"

"He got moved," Caelyn said.

"Moved?" To a different house? Were there other houses like Faetre?

"Downstairs. He turned fifteen. And he's brilliant."

"Wow," I managed. He would do such a good job. And he wouldn't be sent to the front lines. He would get to stay here, under steel and concrete, safe.

But I pictured him running and playing outside; the grown-ups didn't have playtime.

Annevi twisted her fork around on her plate instead of eating.

Which I realized was what I had been doing. I took a few bites of our beans on toast.

Some of the boys seemed almost cheerful. Maybe they liked knowing that they'd be able to move downstairs later. Maybe some of them were hoping to become the top kid, like Tommy had been.

A few seemed down, but not like Annevi.

After lunch, I didn't go back to the soldier. I didn't see the point. I milled about the living room with everyone else, watching Fredericka read and Gunnar determine whether his family might be bombed, Brid and Caelyn find their patterns and Hamlin pace between the tables giving orders as Tommy had been doing only yesterday, and Annevi shift her ships more slowly than usual.

As soon as we got outside, Tyssia Tag started up. Annevi ran with the others, but she didn't try to tackle anyone. I stayed behind her, so she couldn't see me.

And then I ran at her, launching myself up onto her shoulders and throwing her all the way to the ground, landing on top of her. I untied and stole her sea-colored armband.

The breath knocked out of her, she rolled over to see who had brought her down.

She looked surprised to see me. She saw her stolen armband, dangling before her eyes, and took in the tiger stripes on my own arm.

Would she get angry?

Or would she play along?

She let out a shriek and pushed me off of her. She scrambled to her feet and launched herself at me as I ran away.

She would play.


The next day I went back to the cell.

A prison cell for a prisoner.

With a small section for me.

I was a prisoner, too.

After three days, I really should have had something to tell to the Examiner. She'd pulled me aside, but I'd had nothing to say.

Mostly I was tired of sitting in someone's presence, not talking.

On the fourth day of sitting and staring at the wall, boredom was about to drive me crazy.

At least I got to leave the terrible little room. Rainer had to stay there all the time.

But . . . the bombed streets back home, that terrible wailing . . . he deserved it.

He could sit here forever and rot, as far as I was concerned.

Staring at him, with his cold, unfeeling manner, I didn't blame Annevi for not minding if they blew up the ships she found.

But still, the silence wore on me, and I couldn't understand why it wasn't bothering him, too.

I asked, "Where do you come from?"

I asked, "How old are you?"

"Do you have a family?"

"Did you go to school?"

"What do you eat, where you're from?"

"Is it cold there?"

"What's your favorite season?"

"What's your favorite color?"

Nothing.


At Tyssia Tag, Hamlin tackled me and stole my armband.

The next day, Annevi snatched my armband without even needing to tackle me.

The day after that, Fredericka, who never plays, got my band.

Whichever side I was on, was guaranteed to lose.


"How is it going?" the Examiner asked for the tenth time.

Her office was another place I wished I spent less time, though it was really only a few minutes a day.

I wanted to say "Fine," but I couldn't. "Nothing's happening."

"That's all right. Just try again tomorrow."

But what would be different?

"How—how did we get Rainer?" I had figured out that Rainer must have been brought here on the day of our outing.

The Examiner paused, deciding whether to tell me. Eventually, she said, "Rainer was captured in the mountains on our side of the border. Nine others were with him."

"Where are the others?"

"They didn't make it."

"Oh."

Even if it sounded like you were lucky, it felt awful to be the only one to make it. Like it hurt Caelyn to have been the only one to get better from the flu. And it hurt me to be the only one to leave Lykkelig. "Does Rainer know?"

"He does."

"So . . . we killed the rest of them?"

"Not necessarily. The Tyssians don't view it as honorable to be captured. They would rather die than be prisoners, than risk talking about their country's secrets."

"I can't get him to tell me anything." I didn't want to say she'd made a mistake again. But she seemed to be waiting for me to talk. I took a deep breath. "Father said to help end the war and come home. Everyone else is helping. They find ships and defend cities. I can't do anything at all. Maybe that's why you gave me this job. You didn't want to waste anybody else on something impossible."

I sat stiffly in the chair in front of her desk, but she seemed at ease on the other side. After a few silent moments, she spoke.

"Tell me, what did Annevi bring from home?"

"I— What?"

"What did Annevi bring from home?"

"She never told me."

"Think. You each brought something special from home. What would you guess Annevi brought?"

I thought about Annevi's competitiveness, how she wanted to move right on to the next assignment after finishing one, how much she concentrated, how she usually played tag as if it was as serious as her job.

"Maybe ... maybe a little medal for something she did well at? Like a little prize from school?"

"And Caelyn, what do you think she brought?"

Caelyn, whose parents and brothers were gone. Who wondered if there were untold reasons she had been sent away.

"A photo of her family, if she had one."

"What did our prisoner bring from home?"

"Nothing. He wasn't allowed to keep anything."

"Wrong. Find out what he brought from home."

I must have looked puzzled, because she said, "I think it will go best if you just be yourself."

What did she mean? I'd already asked him everything I could think of.

"How about Gunnar? What did Gunnar bring from home?"

My answer stuck in my throat, because I was about to say that Gunnar brought his heart from home.

The Examiner smiled at me. "You're dismissed. For today."


On the next day of silence, when I stood to leave, I paused before exiting. Despite being so angry at him, for what his country had done, for remaining silent while I sat with him day after day, I thought about how it felt to be the only one. To be left behind. I thought about how I'd helped Annevi by showing her that I could play, too, Gunnar by admitting I worried, too. By offering myself.

I said, "I like green."

And then on the day after that, when I got up to leave, I heard behind me, "I like blue."

# 23

*I LIKE BLUE.*
*I like blue.*
*I like blue.*

I carried the sentence with me through the rest of the day and the evening, turned it in my head as I lay in bed that night.

It was still there in the morning, when I woke to pull back my black curtains and saw that the sky was mostly gray, but there was a thin blueness to it anyway, that kind that comes with a chilly morning.

*I like blue.*

After breakfast, I let myself into Rainer's room and sat down.

I watched him sitting.

We didn't acknowledge each other.

I pulled my knees to my chest and wrapped my arms around them.

After a few minutes, I said, "My father ..."

I paused, to see if he was listening.

I figured that he was.

"Father works at the post office. He has a beard that's starting to turn gray, and eyes the blue of the sky when the blue is thin, like just after the sun comes up on a cold morning. He calls me Big, because I am the oldest. I used to help him at work in the afternoons. I could sort the letters or go on deliveries with him. But they made new rules about post office security because of the . . ." I looked at him. We both knew. "Because of the war."

I told him about Mother.

And Kammi and Tye.

I did not say *But I'm worried you have killed them.*

I told him about school.

And Megs.

I did not say *It's your fault I do not go to school anymore. It's your fault I'm not with my family and Megs.*

I did not say I had folded them all up like tiny pieces of paper and stowed them in a little box, deep inside me, so I didn't have to think of them and hurt.

I kept all the angry thoughts stuck in my chest, even though they stewed all the while.

Even though they were also true.

I told him about the woods that I loved.

The summer.

The raspberry-glazed buns.


I fell silent. Silent like snow falling: gentle, but building.

Would he answer eventually, like with the colors?

He wiggled his toes—he had no shoes on, just socks, though his laceless boots lay in the corner, but he wasn't going anywhere anyway—and watched his feet.

He looked angry.

As if listening to me had hurt somehow.

But it shouldn't have.

I'd held back all the things I thought would hurt.

I hadn't said anything mean.

Maybe he'd answer me later.

Like with the colors.

I let go of my knees, getting up to leave.

"Those are all things that you have stolen from Tyssia."

His words fell through my mind slowly, like stones plopping into a stream: I heard them one at a time.

"What?"

"All those things—the raspberries, the woods, the stream, the mushrooms—those belong to Tyssians."

A hot pit grew in my stomach.

What should I say?

It was my job to talk to him. And he was finally ready. I couldn't leave now.

*Remain calm. See what he needs to say.*

See what I could learn.

I took a deep breath and spoke slowly.

"My home is in Sofarende. All those things are within Sofarende. Why would you say they belong to you?"

"You took them from us."

He was crazy.

"Of course we didn't."

"You did. Where you live is the ancestral home of Tyssians."

"But we've been here for hundreds of years."

"But half of your land was home to Tyssians. You have not been Sofarende for hundreds of years. Less than one hundred years. On stolen land."

Each province had voted to become one country called Sofarende. The Sofarers, Tyssians, Eileans, and Nor'landers . . . everyone had blended together to be modern Sofarenders.

We hadn't kept track of who was who.

We hadn't seen a reason to.

We had been proud to be mixed.

I *could* have been part Tyssian by blood; I lived in southern Sofarende, where it was more likely. And I looked like Rainer.

It had never mattered before. Never even entered a discussion.

My skin crawled.

"They voted," I said. "The Tyssians in those areas wanted to become part of Sofarende."

"There must have been someone threatening them to do so."

"I don't remember learning about any threats."

"You wouldn't. Why would they have taught you that at school? If you've even been to school. You seem to just sit around all day."

"For someone who hasn't wanted to talk for days, you sure have a lot to say." I glared at him.

"For someone who tried to get me to talk for days, you should be glad I am telling you what I know."

"The only things stolen are the things you've taken from us since this war began—including the lives of the innocent people you've bombed in their sleep."

"*I* didn't bomb anyone."

"And what about the Skaven lands? They don't have Tyssian ancestors. How did you justify taking them?"

Rainer's eyes went glazed and empty. He turned away.

No amount of questioning was going to get anything else out of him today.

Not that it mattered.

He was a liar.

# 24

"YES, WE'D HEARD FROM people on the ground that they'd been saying that." The Examiner folded her hands in front of her on her desk.

"You have—people—on the ground? You mean, inside Tyssia?"

"Of course we do."

"Then what do you need me for?"

"You are angry?"

"No, I just—I just—I don't understand."

"We have lots of people who work for us, who help us. What else did he have to say?"

"That we threatened the Tyssians who voted to be part of Sofarende a hundred years ago. That's not—that's not true, is it?"

"How did you feel, when you heard that?"

I clenched my jaw; that was probably answer enough. "Is it true?"

"No, it's not true. Sometimes it doesn't matter how long you've been somewhere. Before that, always, the land belonged to someone else. Or was shared by someone else. That's true almost everywhere."

"So Tyssia's *not* right."

"They're right that there was a history of Tyssian people living here. But they weren't threatened into voting a certain way. We have a long tradition of open and fair democracy; we're known for it. He's been presented with a version of history his government chooses for him, to convince him that there's a reason to fight us. Really, we think they want our sea access and to pose a bigger threat to Eilean's empire."

"So they don't have a claim to this land?"

"A lot of peoples could put historical claim on this land. On any land. It just depends on how far back you want to go."

I nodded.

She leaned forward. "His belief that he is right—that is one thing he brought from home."

The next day, I went up to Rainer's cell with my arms full. I passed the items carefully through the bars. While our fingers wouldn't touch, I was able to get things through far enough for him to reach them and draw them over to his side.

First, a scroll of paper. He unfurled it, turned it over; both sides were blank. He looked back toward me.

I held up three paintbrushes.

He nodded.

I reached through with the brushes, and then tried to hand him the small tubes of paint, but they weren't long enough to get through the gaps, so I ended up tossing them so they landed on his side, and he reached through to retrieve them.

"I'm sorry," I said. "I can't easily get you the rest of the things."

"It is okay," he said. "I will use my dishes."

He got his empty breakfast plate, squeezed out and mixed the colors. Set to work.

I knelt by the fence, watching.

Brown with jagged streaks of red and black. And an orange glow.

Like the nights of bombing.

It wasn't fond memories of home that he'd decided to paint.

Rainer filled the paper quickly.

Then he rested on his heels, looking at it.

"I'll be right back," I said.

I ran to the art room and grabbed sheets and sheets of paper. Arriving back in his room moments later, I scrolled them up as I had the first one and passed them to him.

He nodded, and painted and painted. The images and colors took shape a little more—I could make out a sort of wheeled warcraft, the khaki-beige outfits of his comrades, faces black with mud but with eyes stark white—swishes of orange added into the red showed fire—white and black together showed smoke—black naked trees, stems of what would have once been thriving with life, burnt and ruined.

Paper after paper lined the floor.

Then he suddenly stopped painting.

My heart was pounding.

His brow and upper lip dripped with sweat; his breath

came in uneven gasps, as if he had been running through those fields and their smoke just now, finding no refreshing leaves to cool him, only the machines of war.

He looked at me for just a second, as if I passed into his thoughts only momentarily, then back at the pages. He made a roar from deep in his throat and picked up one of them, about to twist his hands in opposite directions.

"Wait!"

I threw myself against the fence, my fingers gripping the wire hexagons.

"Don't. Don't ruin them."

"They are garbage. It's all garbage. Everything is garbage."

"I—I want them. I'll take them out of here, but, please, just let them dry."

"You are my captor. You made me do this. You are in charge. If you say so, I will not destroy them, but I won't look at them anymore."

He dropped the painting, went to the wall farthest from me, and stood with his head against it.

"I am *not* your captor."

"You keep me here. You have keys. You could let me go."

"I have keys only for this side. I didn't lock you up."

"But you think I deserve to be locked up."

"I've seen the houses of people I know bombed to bits. It looks like what you've painted. And you did that to us."

"Not *me*. My country. And only to reclaim what was ours."

"It wasn't *yours*. You're only believing what you've been told."

"Maybe you're only believing what you've been told!" He turned around. "You're just a stupid little girl anyway. You have space and food that belongs to Tyssians, that we need!"

"You're the ones who've cut off *our* food."

I sat down with my back to the fence. The hexagons pressed into me; under my thin sweater and my blouse, they made their imprints, which would stay on my skin for far too long.

I turned to find him sitting with his back against his fence, as I had been, the same hexagons pressing into his back through the big red X on his clothes.

"Were you really hungry, before?" I asked.

He didn't answer.

"You made my family afraid for our house and for our lives. You made my parents send me away. I don't even know if they or my sisters are still alive. I may never see them again. You understand?"

He nodded.

Maybe he would never see his own family again. And maybe he had thought that he should go in order for them to have enough to eat.

*No!*

I pushed those thoughts away.

"We—me and my family—did nothing to deserve that, no matter what someone told you about the past."

He nodded again.

I knelt on my side of the fence, my head level with his.

We each believed it was the other's fault we were in this room.

# 25

I WALKED THROUGH AN open space, an uncertain landscape of odd slashes of red and brown and black.

A road formed beneath my feet, the gritty gravel looking sharp at first, then fuzzy, then sharp again, as it crunched beneath my steps.

I looked up; the landscape had been brushed through with a smeary gray, changing all the forms, as if wind tugged at their edges, making them indistinct and drifting.

And only when I thought *wind* did I feel it on my skin, whipping roughly by, raising up a howling noise.

Up ahead, on the road, a figure started to take shape, first built out of the grayness itself, but with dark gashes indicating eyes and mouth. Then brown hair became visible, and, in a surprising splash of color, a green cap.

"Father!"

The wind tore my breath from me.

"Father!"

But the fuzzy face turned, the figure stepped and shrank, moving away from me.

"NO!"

He would disappear into the great swirl of color and rush of noise; he would no longer exist.

"Wait!"

I fixed my eyes on the green cap, somehow growing dimmer and smaller as I ran toward it, my feet shoving the black gravel as I hurtled.

He was smaller, then bigger; nearer, then farther.

"Father! Wait! It's me! It's Mathilde!"

Finally he was within inches, his back still turned to me.

"Wait!"

I threw my hand out, and, while it looked as if my hand touched his elbow, I felt only air and that terrible whipping wind.

And when he turned to me, the features of his face were still black gashes, and they expanded to engulf him—until he disintegrated.

"No! Wait!"


My own screaming woke me up.

But as I came to, sweaty and thrashing in the immense darkness, a figure appeared in front of me.

I might have reached out, but fear that he or she was made of only wisps gripped me.

"It's Annevi."

"Oh," I choked. "Annevi."

My mind filled in her form, sitting at the end of my bed, and, though my heart was still thudding hard, my panic faded.

"Why are you in my room?"

"You were screaming. For your father."

"I'm sorry for waking you."

"You didn't. I was up already."

She hadn't tried to wake me, or comfort me. She was just observing me as if mildly curious.

My neck was hot and sweaty. I'd soaked my pillow.

"You aren't the only one who screams at night, you know."

"No?"

"No."

"Do you go into their rooms?"

"Not usually."

"Why mine, then?"

"You sounded particularly terrified."

"Well—good." Why didn't she just go away? The show was over.

"What happened?" she asked.

Not to soothe.

Because she was curious.

I fell back against my pillow.

The wind, the swirling colors . . .

It hurt even to try to grasp it again—setting my head and my heart tight and racing.

Even if she didn't intend to help me, that didn't mean that it wouldn't help me to talk about it.

As the dream warped even further, I tried to recall it. To explain.

"I couldn't catch him. I couldn't hold on to him."

"Your father?"

"Yes."

When we'd both been silent for a short time, Annevi moved to stand up.

"Wait." The word caught in my throat, as if I was still in the dream, trying fruitlessly to shout it. "Stay—stay with me."

Annevi sat back down.

She didn't touch me, she didn't tell me it would be all right or even that she, too, worried about people from home, but curled up like a cat at the end of my bed.

For the first time since I'd left home, I fell asleep to the sound of someone else breathing.

# 26

A REAL CAT MIGHT have wandered away in the night, but Annevi was still there when I woke and pulled up the black curtain.

She even stretched like a cat, and was still for a moment, looking around, remembering where she was.

"What are those?" she asked, taking in the one decoration in the room.

"Our handprints. Mine and my sisters'."

"I don't have sisters."

I wanted to smooth her rumpled hair, but I didn't. I'd never seen Annevi touch someone that way, gently; she always played so rough.

"Annevi? What did you bring from home?"

She paused for a minute. "I won a race once. Best in the school. Even better than the older boys. They gave me a medal for it."

Something in my core went warm and cold at once.

"Congratulations."

"Thanks. I wish they had races for us here."

"You should tell the Examiner. I bet she'd like that idea."

"The who?"

"The Examiner."

"*Who?*"

"You know, the woman in charge."

"Miss Markusen?"

Was that her name? I must have missed it when she introduced herself to the children lined up for the test, because I was late, talking with Kammi. And she must have told my parents, when she was taking away their daughter. I hadn't been listening.

"Why do you call her that?" Annevi asked.

"Because she gave us the examination, I guess."

And she had been examining us ever since.

Annevi stayed quietly beside me for our morning walk, but she left to eat with Tommy, who had come to breakfast with us after an overnight shift, and Hamlin.

I peeled my boiled egg slowly, and ate it with big gulps of milk between bites.

Thoughts of going to talk to Rainer seemed like re-entering the bad dream.

But after breakfast, I marched myself to the second floor, unlocked the door, and entered.

His paintings, now dry and warped, lay between the fencing. When I slid them to my side, they crinkled and crackled.

Rainer sat, knees up, in his own corner, his breakfast untouched. He, too, had a boiled egg, though his glass was filled with water rather than milk.

Milk was for children. Especially these days.

Even the egg seemed generous, as there weren't a lot of those, either.

Generous to give a prisoner.

The enemy.

Dark circles surrounded Rainer's eyes, as if he had been up the whole night crying. As if his dreams had been as colored by the paintings as mine had been.

But that wasn't right.

The paintings hadn't colored his dreams; his dreams had colored the paintings.

He wasn't much older than Tommy, after all.

"You should eat your egg," I said.

He looked at me.

"You should eat your egg."

He picked it up, cradling it, warm and smooth, in his hands. Then he gave it a brisk knock on the floor and started peeling it. He made it last six bites, and finished up with a swallow of water.

I studied his paintings. Something that looked like a house appeared in many of them.

"Is that your house?" I asked.

He didn't answer.

That wouldn't have made sense, for it to be his house.

If he had been fighting on the ground . . . "Were you in the Skaven lands?"

He knew I was there—of course he did, he had eaten the egg when I told him to. It was the opposite—he was making a point of knowing I was there, but choosing not to acknowledge me.

Which was an acknowledgement in itself.

He lowered his head, still making as if he was ignoring me.

My own dreams wouldn't go away.

Chasing, and failing to catch, Father.

Mother, Kammi, and Tye, Megs—all twisted red and black and gray as if burnt.

I wandered a road through blackened trees, or hollow shells of buildings, back on the bombed streets of Lykkelig. Looking for our house, which didn't seem to be anywhere.

I went to see Rainer a few times, but we didn't speak.

I stopped going so much.

I trailed through the living room instead.

Brid and Caelyn asked me to sit with them, but one afternoon Caelyn slid my papers back in front of her when I was staring into space instead of marking them.

She also finished my dinner for me, when I couldn't eat it.

The next morning I plopped onto a couch in the living room, not even pretending to do anything.

Gunnar eventually came over. "Mathilde?"

I stared at him.

"Lykkelig was okay last night."

I rested my head back on the armrest.

"Do you want to come help us?"

He stood there, waiting for me to answer.

"No!" I yelled, sitting up. "I don't want to talk about who's being bombed!"

Gunnar walked away.

When he returned, he had the Examiner with him.

She sat down next to me on the couch and felt my forehead.

"Thank you, Gunnar," she said. He went back to his group and sat down. "Did you find out something?"

"No."

"Are you sure? Something's changed. Something's upset you."

I didn't know if it was the kind of information she wanted, but it was the only thing I could think of. "I got Rainer to paint."

She raised her eyebrows.

I brought the paintings to the Examiner's office.

She looked me over carefully, fixing on my face.

Could she see the dark circles under my eyes? I must have had them when she met me at school and when I arrived here; they had faded only to reappear.

When she was done looking me over, she turned to the paintings.

"Thank you very much," she said, as if I had just given her a thoughtful birthday present, one that touched her.

"There's a house—or something, a building—that shows up again and again."

"Yes, I see. Do you know anything more about it?"

"No."

"Maybe you could find out? And also what his mission was in Sofarende."

I sighed. "I can try."

"Are you sure you're well, Mathilde?"

"Yes," I said, but my voice did not come out very strong.

## 27

THE EXAMINER DISAPPEARED for a few days.

Had she gone on a mission? Was she recruiting new kids?

I didn't have any news about Rainer anyway.

But then she was back, and just after lunch, she pulled me aside.

"Anything new to report?"

I shook my head.

"I don't want you to visit Rainer this afternoon. Or be in the main room. I would like you to spend the afternoon in your own room."

We didn't get sent to our rooms. Was I being punished?

I sat on my bed with a book. After a while, I started to feel sleepy. It was easier, safer, to feel sleepy in the daylight.

While I dozed sitting up, my door flew open and arms squeezed my middle, a dark head of long, braided hair pressing into me.

Holding me so tight.

With so much love I could burst.

• • •

I must have fallen asleep.

Or maybe we'd been bombed. It was all over, and this was what came after life. Visiting those we loved.

Did that mean that she was gone from life, as well?

And finally she turned her face up to look at me.

I ran my thumb over her eyebrows, down her nose. "Megs."

The daylight insisted it was still afternoon; I was still in my bed, in my room.

Miss Ibsen appeared in the doorway. She had probably been behind Megs the whole time. She shut the door, leaving us alone.

"They cut your hair," Megs said.

I blinked, but she didn't disappear. I blinked again, and she laughed at me.

"What on earth are you doing here?"

"Miss Markusen said they needed more kids after all! I wondered if some of the kids who had gone before had been—well, you know—but my papers had been signed, so what could I do? I still wanted my mother to have the money. I hoped the whole time that I would be going to the same place as you, and as soon as I got here they said, 'Mathilde's here, we'll take you to see her,' as if they knew I had been waiting to hear just that!"

Did she smell like the woods in Lykkelig? Was that possible after a journey? I ran my fingers down each of her braids. "They'll cut yours, too, you know. How is everyone? My family? Your family?"

"Everybody's all right! Your parents brought us food

baskets whenever they could. Now that I'm here, they won't need to anymore. But . . ."

"But what?"

"They're thinking of leaving. Everyone's talking about how much longer the borders can hold. The trouble is, no one knows where to go."

The only safe place I knew was Faetre.

"So what do you do here?" Megs asked.

"I . . ."

But Miss Ibsen opened the door again.

"Come on, Megs. It's time to cut your hair. And then you can wash up, if you like."

Megs got up and headed to the door. She must have felt the same nerves I had on my first day, wanting to start off on the right foot.

As Miss Ibsen led Megs away, I followed her as far as the hallway.

The Examiner was standing there.

I flung my arms around her.

She let me hug her, and when I pulled back, she placed her hand under my chin and tipped my face up toward hers.

"Ah, there it is. Some of the blue had gone out of your eyes. But it's back." She let go.

"But you said—before—that Megs—?"

"Megs will serve us well here, no need to think otherwise. Now, run along and join them, you look as though you're in need of a trim. When Megs is ready, you can help her find something to do."

# 28

HAIR CUT, MEGS WAS once again my opposite-twin. I led her by the hand to the living room. I just couldn't let her go!

As Megs looked around, I remembered my first day and Annevi asking what I was good at.

Megs was good at learning things, so she could probably work anywhere.

Where would she most like to be?

I led her to Brid and Caelyn, who looked up at us.

"This is Megs. We'd like to help you."

The girls nodded, and each slid over half a stack of papers and pushed extra pencils into the middle of the table. Brid explained to Megs what to look for. By the end of the hour and the call to dinner, Megs had found twice as many things to mark as I had.

But I was glad about that.

Changed into our nightclothes, we lay in my bed. I kept squeezing her feet, propped by my head on the pillow.

"I'm still here," she said.

"I keep forgetting."

"You're not forgetting. You're just having trouble believing."

"Tell me about home."

Megs thought. "Your father found a bicycle. A broken one, but he fixed it up. Kammi learned to ride it. Tye *thinks* she learned to ride it, but her feet don't reach the pedals; your father makes the bike go."

That sounded like Father.

We talked so late that we both fell asleep in my room.

For the first night in a long time, I didn't have any nightmares.

We didn't need coats for our morning walk. The trees were so green, leaves dancing. The air smelled so fresh.

The sky looked so blue.

I left Megs with Brid and Caelyn again, but it was still my job to go and see Rainer.

I stopped at the art room on the way, let myself into the cell, and sat down.

Rainer looked up.

"What has happened?"

"What do you mean?"

"You are . . . happy."

"My friend is here!"

"Oh?"

"Megs. Megs, who I told you about."

"Oh yes. Megs. You are glad she is well?"

"Very glad." My smile faded as I looked into his sad face. "Do you . . . do you know where your friends are?"

Rainer tugged at his boot tongues. "Some of them went to battle with me. We signed up in groups, went in together. Some of them did not make it. The rest, I don't know."

"You had to sign up? You chose to or you had to?"

"There was no difference. Everything was about fighting for Tyssia, and if you said that you didn't want to, you could be beat up, or sent away, or your property given away. Your family would starve. You had no choice, but it had to look like you chose."

Like Father and street patrol.

I stood up and went to the fence. I passed the things from the art room through it. "Paint me something else."

He collected the single sheet of paper, the paint tubes. "These are all blue."

"I know. I want you to paint me something blue."

Rainer shrugged and set to work. He took a lot longer with the blue paints, testing the shades, adding touches here and there. The image emerged slowly, upside down from where I watched.

An hour or so had passed by the time Rainer stopped painting.

"Can I see?" I asked.

He looked calmer than I'd ever seen him as he handed the paper to me through the fence.

Unlike Rainer's other paintings of jagged slashes, the blue painting consisted of soft lines, hues blended together to make shapes with light, rather than darkness.

The center of the image was an open space surrounded by a river, buildings, and fields. There were people everywhere.

"Is this a real place?" I asked. "Are they real people?"

165

"It is the village where I grew up. Or it is meant to be. It is not easy to make what you imagine come out right in paints."

"I know. What are all the people doing?"

"On the weekly day off, women did the washing in the river. Near the river were poles where the families would hang out their rugs and the children would beat them clean. The men would go around to each other's houses and fix things, chairs and tables, doorframes and roof shingles. Everyone brought food to share and we'd have a picnic while the clothes dried on lines. Everyone helped everyone else."

A lump grew in my throat. I couldn't tell if it was because I was happy or sad.

"It looks like you grew up in a very nice place," I managed to say.

"It was nice, once."

If Tyssia was so nice, why had they wanted to start a war?

I stood up to leave. "Thank you ... for your painting. And for telling me about your home." I started toward the door.

"Mathilde?"

I turned back.

"Have fun with your friend."

His eyes bored through me.

Sincere.

"Thanks."


When I joined the others in the main room before lunch, they were all gathered around one table, except for a few children, who were at the telephones, furiously jotting things down.

This would be either very good news, or very bad news.

One of the boys from the telephones read out new numbers, and a girl added pins to the table.

It was a map of Sofarende. The pins stuck out of several sites at odd angles.

"What happened?" I asked Gunnar.

"They're bombing our aerstrips."

"In the daytime?"

He nodded. The other kids were still, waiting.

The proctors hovered on the outskirts of the group. They looked anxious, arms folded or hands to their faces as if in thought, but they didn't interrupt us or make suggestions.

As if they wanted to see what we could do, on our own.

"But why didn't someone see the aerials coming? Aren't there telephones out there, to pass the messages, so the next aerstrips could get ready?" a girl asked. It sounded like she had already asked. Like she couldn't believe it.

"Maybe they were warned but Tyssia's getting through anyway," Annevi said.

"We know their flight patterns," Hamlin said. "They always have fighters and then the bombers right behind. We should be ready for that."

Megs bit her lower lip. She caught my eye, and I nodded to her.

"Last week ..." She paused, not expecting anyone to listen.

But everyone was. They all looked at her, waiting.

"Last week, the formation looked ... different. It looked more like a V."

"How do you know?" Hamlin asked.

"She watched the aerials at night," I whispered. "Over Lykkelig."

Without me there, had she stopped bothering to go down to the basement at all?

A few people looked at me, but most of them looked quickly back at Megs. Hamlin, who had gone a bit pale, marched over to one of the free telephones.

"Megs," Hamlin said after a minute, extending the earpiece to her. "Tell them. They'll listen."

Megs took the telephone and spoke into it quietly. They must have been asking her questions, because she would pause sometimes before speaking again.

"Can someone mark the other aerstrips, the ones that *haven't* been hit yet?" Megs called to the group.

Gunnar and the other boys who did bombing predictions grabbed black pins and pushed them into the board, scattered over the country, but mostly near Tyssia's border.

"They want to know where you think they'll go next."

Gunnar and the others all talked and pointed at once. Much faster than usual, they decided a color code of pins and pushed them in, reaching over and across one another to label the aerfields for their strategic advantages. In a few minutes, the smattering of pins had clumped around some aerfields more than others.

Gunnar ran to Megs at the telephone. She stepped aside as he breathlessly recited their guesses at the next five targets.

We were not called to lunch. Trays of sandwiches were brought in, and pitchers of water, so we could help ourselves while we marked updates on the map, coming up with strategies and ideas, reporting downstairs.

But playtime was not optional. As always. There was a

lot of grumbling as the Examiner came in to insist that we go outside.

There was no Tyssia Tag. No chasing. Nobody wanted to play.

Nobody wanted to be chased.

I linked arms with Megs and we marched through the trees and came back around to the main clearing. We didn't speak, our minds on things that were far away. Other kids looked up at the sky, as if expecting aerials to emerge at any moment. Some drew in the dirt with sticks, plotting new strategies, only to scuff them out and start over.

Finally we were called back inside, but there still wasn't anything to do but wait. People tried to get back to their usual tasks, but nobody could focus.

Just before dinner, a uniformed officer came upstairs to speak with us.

"I want to thank you for your help today. While they hit eight of our aerstrips, and dozens of our aerials, we managed to prevent bombings at three more targeted aerfields and chased them on their retreat. They failed to land and take any of our aerstrips, and we shot down all of their remaining craft. None of them made it back over the border."

Hamlin cheered first. Many people joined in and clapped. Kids were giving Megs light punches on her arms and shoulders. Biscuits appeared from somewhere, and colored paper for making hats and chains.

I stayed put in the armchair I'd been in before the announcement.

A while later, Gunnar plopped into the chair across from mine.

"I made you . . . a hat!" He pulled it out from behind his

back. It had great plumes of blue and green, reminding me of the wave-crest symbol for Sofarende.

My favorite color, with Rainer's.

I took the hat and twisted it round and round in my hands.

"Young people fly the aerials. They're just like—"

"Like . . . ?"

". . . and none of them made it home."

Someone had found a music player and turned on a recording.

"Dance?"

I shook my head.

"At least put on your hat." He took it back from me and set it on my head. "I crown you queen of Sofarende."

"We don't have a queen."

"Exactly. There was an opening. Now, what shall we call you? Queen Mathilde the Kind?"

I kept shaking my head.

"Fine. Queen Mathilde the Resolute it is."

I finally smiled. "I'm sorry I yelled at you. The other day."

"That's okay." Gunnar dropped his voice. "I *do* understand, you know."

"I know."


Megs came to my room again that night, bathed and in her nightclothes, still flushed happy pink. She flopped onto my bed opposite me, mirroring my position, staring up at the ceiling.

"Good job today," I told her.

"Thanks. Who was that . . . boy . . . you were with?"

"Gunnar. It's not like that."

"No?"

"Don't you think I would have told you?"

"I don't know. There seem to be a lot of things you haven't told me."

"What are you talking about?"

She propped herself on her elbow to face me. "Like where were you today? When everything started happening?"

"I was . . . working on my assignment. Like everyone else."

"Well—where? What *is* your assignment?"

"I go upstairs and . . . I . . ."

"See?" She lay back down. "I could help you."

Would she do a better job at it than me? Probably, but they obviously needed her in the main room.

"Fine, have secrets."

"You had them first."

"I didn't!"

"You did! Like why you were always late to the Hellers', watching the aerials. And that you were going to take the test."

"You can't pretend you didn't know that, if you had wanted to admit it. And it all worked out anyway, didn't it? I promised I would be with you, and I am now. So *let* me be with you."

I bit my lip. "I would *like* to tell you. I'll see if I can."

# 29

IN THE MORNING, I went to the Examiner's office.

"Come in, Mathilde. What did you want to see me about?"

"I have some questions. About Rainer."

"Ah. Sit down."

I sat.

"Is Rainer . . . a secret?"

"From whom?"

"The . . . others."

"The other children, you mean?"

"Yes."

"I expect you to be discreet, but if you want to tell someone, I'm sure that you will do so in the right way, and for the right reasons."

I nodded. "And also . . . I'm still not sure why you've assigned me to Rainer."

"I had wanted to see if the two of you could relate to each other. If he would tell someone like you more than he would tell someone like me. And he has. You've gotten a picture of his mind. You've found his beliefs and hopes, their strengths and gaps. We can use things like that on him and other soldiers to win them over. Or break them."

It was like Annevi's ships. Or Brid and Caelyn's codes. Or shooting down aerials. I'd hand over what I knew and let the grown-ups decide what to do with it.

"You mean you might use it to hurt people. Rainer, or other people like him." My cheeks grew hot. "You're using us. You use all of us."

The Examiner spoke gently. "You have every right to be angry."

While I seethed, she went on. "We hope you will all see your work as part of our goals of keeping you safe, helping you survive the war."

"But you only take kids you think will be useful to you! If you really wanted to save children, you would help everyone, whether they passed your stupid test or not!"

"If I could hide every child in Sofarende here, I would. If I could send you all to live in safety on an island far away, I would. Children have no place in war."

"But I thought—but you've asked us to—"

She smiled. "Some of us here thought, what if that idea could play out the opposite way? What if we could get children out of the war by giving them a place in it? We don't have the resources to save everyone, Mathilde. I wish we did. For every single one of you that we take, we have to justify the choice. Your gifts have saved you, and we hope you can help us save others. We take those of you we think will be the most help to Sofarende, to everyone."

Was this that objective thinking the way Gunnar had

meant it? Or was this protecting one's own all over again, just making excuses for it?

"But you still choose to protect some people over others, for your own reasons. There were people like that at home, too; there were people like—"

"Like you?" Her eyes flashed, narrowing in on me.

The words hit the center of my chest like a punch. It hurt to breathe.

"When you begged me to let someone else take your place to come here, you asked that a specific, single person take your place. You did not ask that I take everyone, or just anyone. You were protecting the person who meant the most to you. You behaved selflessly—you almost missed the test to comfort your sister; you left the test to comfort your friend—but your sister and your best friend are not just anyone, are they?"

My heart swelled with love for Kammi and Megs, and my mind struggled to defend it as hot shame flooded my chest.

Was I as guilty as the others, the ones I'd talked to Mother about? The ones who'd shut us out when we'd needed kindness?

A tear escaped.

Could tears burn you?

Miss Markusen came around to my side of the desk. She knelt and gently wiped away the tear, and the ones that came splashing after it, with a clean, soft, baby-blue handkerchief.

"That is the best start, Mathilde, to learn to love. It will help you see that every person matters, that everyone is someone's loved one."

Gunnar had said that to me. He was better at this than I was.

"The truth is, you already do. You think so carefully about how things affect people. That's why our work here is so hard for you. And it's why we need you.

"We all have to make difficult choices. If we make the right ones, hopefully they will allow others to make more right ones, and, one day, things will get better."

When I finally looked back up at the Examiner, she said, "We are trying to make the world a safe place. You have to trust us, Mathilde. We trust you."

# 30

MEGS AND I SAT together at lunch, though we were both very quiet. It took me the whole meal to get out the sentence I needed to say.

"Come with me."

"Okay."

On the way out of the lunchroom, I caught Gunnar's elbow.

"Come with us?"

"Where?"

"You'll see."

Making sure no one followed us, I led them up the stairs and along the hallway to my door to Rainer's room. I took the key in my hand, and just held it.

My friends waited.

"My assignment here ... I spend time with a Tyssian soldier. It's my job to get to know him. To find out what he knows. That's all. I thought you might like to meet him?"

Megs and Gunnar looked at each other.

"I mean, maybe not *like* to. *Would* you come to meet him?"

"There's been a Tyssian here, all this time?" Gunnar asked.

"About as long as I've been here. If you come in, you can talk to him, about anything except our work, okay?"

They both nodded.

"And don't be afraid."

I opened the door, and the three of us stepped inside.

"You brought people to stare at me?" Rainer's eyes opened wider as all three of us filed into my side of the room. He came close to the fence.

"To *meet* you."

"Hello," Megs said in Tyssian.

"It must be true, then, that Sofarenders do not go to school."

"There's a war on," Gunnar said. "We're learning plenty."

Rainer smiled. I relaxed.

"Rainer, these are my friends, Megs and Gunnar."

"Miss Megs. Mathilde told me about you."

"She did?" Megs's cheeks went pink.

"Yes. You have been good friends for a very long time. I have not heard of you, Gunnar."

"I'm . . . new. We met here."

"The mysterious 'here.' Where are we?"

All three of us pressed our lips tight.

"Right. The place no one talks about."

Megs looked at me, and I nodded at her to go ahead.

"What do you want most? To win the war?"

"To go home. I have had enough of the war."

"Us too," Gunnar said.

"But I cannot go home."

"Why not?" Megs asked.

"It is not honorable to have been caught by the enemy. My family will be ashamed of me. If the army found me . . ."

Gunnar, Megs, and I all looked at each other. I could guess by the looks on their faces that, like me, neither of them had thought about not being welcomed home if we got to go back.

Rainer wasn't welcome on either side. He never would be, ever again.

"I'm sorry," Megs said.

"You were captured in Sofarende?" Gunnar asked.

"Yes."

"What were you doing here?"

Rainer looked from one of us to the next. "There's a war on."

Gunnar stared back at him and crossed his arms over his chest, but then he shrugged.

"You go ahead," I said to Megs and Gunnar. "I'll come down soon."

"Goodbye, Miss Megs and Mr. Gunnar. Be glad you Sofarenders do not go to school."

Megs and Gunnar didn't know Rainer well enough to see the change that came over his eyes as he said that. It happened so quickly.

After they left, Rainer looked at me.

"Do Sofarenders seem like people who have stolen from you?" I asked.

"Your friends seemed . . . nice."

"The whole world is not there for you to take. You have to let other people have a part of it."

Rainer sighed. We both sat down in our usual spots. We were quiet for a little while.

"What did you mean, about 'be glad' we don't go to school?"

At first, Rainer did nothing. Then he covered his face with his hands.

"What is it?"

I waited.

Finally he said, "In the Skaven lands . . . they made us burn down a school."

I stared at him. He didn't move. He kept his face covered.

"Why?"

"The schoolmaster, he would not follow the rules. He would not conduct the school day in Tyssian. He would not teach our Tyssian history. We received orders to make an example of him. . . ."

My heart was pounding. "But, the school was empty, right? Everyone had gone home, right?"

Covering my ears didn't block out his crying. It would echo in my dreams. My nightmares. They rose in my mind again, like when your throat warns you before you throw up.

The nightmares I shared with *him.*

I didn't want to share anything with him!

I scooched backward, pressing against the wall, to get as far away from him as I could.

When I couldn't feel my hands anymore, I dropped

them, letting the blood trickle back on pins and needles. I twisted my cardigan in my lap. Mother always told us not to do that; we'd stretch our sweaters out.

I wanted to lie down. But not in the cell. I needed to get out of the cell.

"You must hate me."

What did he care if I hated him? What did he care about one Sofarender girl?

I didn't know that it was possible for my heart to beat so fast. "What *were* you doing in Sofarende?"

After a while, he said, "Looking for gaps in your border defenses in the mountains. We made it in, but not too far. As you know."

That should have been reassuring, but . . .

"What were you supposed to do after that? After you got in and told others how to get in?"

It was my job to find out.

But wasn't that what Rainer had been doing? His job?

I didn't want to know any more.

I was late for playtime.

I went down the steps, looking around for my friends. No Tyssia Tag. Again.

Gunnar waved. I waved back. We would talk later.

Megs stood waiting for me, hands in her skirt pockets. I headed over to her.

"I'm sorry," she said. "I had no idea. I understand why you had to keep that secret."

"It's all right. The war pulled us apart once already. I wasn't going to let one more soldier come between us."

Megs smiled, but the gentle look in her eyes disappeared quickly. "Mathilde—what's wrong? You're shaking."

I pulled my sweater around me as tight as I could.

"It's not cold out. Did something happen? Did Rainer upset you after we left?"

I nodded, but I couldn't tell her.

He had done that terrible thing. And he lived right here in the building with us, where we ate and slept and played.

Megs squeezed her arm through mine. We walked around the wooded area of Faetre's enclosure.

I could almost pretend we were back home.

As we came out to the clearing again, we could hear it. A low, low rumble at first, then distinct.

My stomach tightened.

We all looked up as a team of tiger-striped aerials zoomed overhead.

For a moment, we all stood still. Then most of the children raced to go back inside.

The Examiner halted us on the steps.

"Stay outside. Keep playing."

A couple of girls gasped.

"They're not bombers," Hamlin explained. "We're okay."

"But where are *our* aerials? Aren't they going to chase them?"

"We need to help!"

"We've given word of these sightings to the right people, but we need your protection now more than ever. Make us look like a school from the air. Annevi, you're it."

Annevi nodded. She hit the girl next to her.

At the same time, Gunnar and Megs declared themselves

it, too, Megs hitting me and Gunnar chasing after someone else. Brid slammed into Caelyn. Hamlin was also it somehow, running in the direction of Annevi to make her it again. I took off. Maybe I could get Hamlin after he got Annevi.

Suddenly we were playing the most furious game of tag in the history of the world.

# 31

I WOKE SEVERAL TIMES in the night, expecting sirens.

And aerial engines.

But waking was better than sleeping.

Sleeping only led to nightmares.

I wished I'd thought to stay with Megs.

I wished Annevi would wander by to check on me.

I wished Faetre still felt safe.

In the morning, I wasn't even tired. I silently trooped through our morning parade around the grounds. Megs stomped along next to me, knowing something was still wrong but not asking what.

I went to the living room with everyone else. I didn't want to see Rainer. Not ever again.

Megs, Brid, and Caelyn settled in to their pages, but I couldn't sit still. I wandered to the bookshelves, sliding out and shoving back every book I touched.

The Examiner came in, started talking with different

children about their work. I watched her move about the room, and I moved, too, always as far away as I could get.

How could she think her plan of us being a school would work?

*She doesn't know. That's why you have to tell her.*

*That's what she wants from you, isn't it?*

My feet marched me over toward her, where she sat speaking softly with Fredericka on a couch. They smiled, poring over some information in the pages of a book in Fredericka's lap.

"You locked me up with a murderer!" I yelled.

They both looked up. Fredericka's mouth fell open as the book tumbled to the floor.

The room went still and quiet.

The one voice that carried on was Hamlin's, reciting a common prayer in Tyssian.

Not praying.

Testing the opening lines of the morning's first coded transmissions for something every Tyssian would know.

The Examiner picked up Fredericka's book and handed it to her. "If you'll excuse me, I think Mathilde needs a few minutes of my time."

She placed a hand on my shoulder, and guided me out of the room. Everyone was looking at me.

She steered me along, but we didn't go to her office.

Were we going somewhere worse? Was she going to punish me for what I'd said in front of everyone?

She didn't take her hand off my shoulder until we were in the kitchen. I'd never been there before. She opened a drawer and took out a spoon. Held it up to me.

It was an awfully small spoon to be punished with.

"I'm not going to hit you. Take it."

I took it.

She led me into a pantry, selected a jar, opened its lid, and set it on the table.

"We don't have your favorite raspberry glaze. Will raspberry jam do?"

I stared at her. "How—"

"Perhaps Megs didn't tell you I took her directly back with me? We rode the train together. She talked a lot."

Megs.

She was probably worried.

My fist tightened around the spoon.

"We won't be safe here, if the Tyssians come, even if we pretend to be a school!"

The Examiner breathed in and out. "I very much want to hear what you have to say, but you need to stop yelling or I won't understand you."

I didn't want to give in and eat the jam, but it shined so pretty red. I dipped my spoon in and had just the littlest bit. It *was* good. The sugar flowed through me as I licked the spoon clean and set it on the table.

"Try again."

I swallowed. "The building in Rainer's paintings . . . it's a school. He had orders to burn it because the schoolmaster wouldn't conduct lessons the way the Tyssians said to. It sounds like . . . there were . . ."

The Examiner looked worried.

She never let us see her look worried.

"Why would he do it?" I asked.

"What do you think would have happened to him if he hadn't?"

"He still didn't—"

"No, think about it."

But I knew what the answer was. If they were making an example of the schoolmaster, they would have done the same thing to their soldiers.

"More than anything, Rainer wants to live. He was afraid to defy his orders. He let himself be captured, even though it was dishonorable. He has as much to fear from the Tyssians as we do. Maybe he'll come around to help us."

I closed my eyes.

I didn't want to think of Rainer as the victim.

He had done awful things.

"How does he feel about what he did?"

His crying had been terrible.

The most desperate I'd ever heard.

# 32

FISTS POUNDED ON MY DOOR. I gasped as I sat up in the dark.

"Coats on! Meet outside!" a boy's voice cried.

Hamlin?

I reached for my coat, feeling along the wall until I came to its hook.

There it was. My fingers fumbled numbly, trying to tug my arms through the sleeves and do up the buttons. I shoved my feet into my shoes.

Were we being bombed? Why would we need coats? The shelter was in the basement.

The pounding fists and call to meet outside continued along the hallway, the noise louder as I opened my door and stepped out among other children, also trying to get their coats on over their nightclothes.

When Hamlin moved on from our hallway, the silence was broken only by the quick slapping of shoes on the floor as we hurried.

A hand grabbed mine.

Megs, of course.

I squeezed back.

Someone found my other hand. Brid. With Caelyn hanging on to her already.

And then we were outside, swept along in the crowd of children.

The night glowed orange and flickering; the air was heavy, smoky.

Like at home, during the bombings.

If we were being bombed, why had they had us come out into the night? They'd promised Mother and Father I'd be under concrete and steel.

We walked onto the grounds toward a large fire, its flames licking high into the night. I looked up at the sky, trying to make out aerials through the smoke.

Nothing.

And no roar of engines.

We weren't being bombed.

Adults were around the fire. But they weren't trying to put out the fire; they were feeding it.

Our mapping tables.

Our charts and codes and papers.

Our books.

Were Tyssians here to burn Faetre?

No. The adults were in Sofarender uniforms and civilian clothes. They were *our* proctors, burning *our* things.

While we watched.

But hadn't our work been important?

As I watched the flames devour it, I realized that was why they *had* to burn it.

So it wouldn't be left.

So nothing would be left.

And there wouldn't be.

Not even us.

We were leaving.

Tyssia wasn't here yet, but they would be.

Pretending to be a school wasn't going to be disguise enough.

It was over.


When I finally looked away from the fire—was it the brightness or the smoke causing my eyes to tear?—and around me at the others, proctors were handing out packets of paper.

When they got to us, Megs and I dropped hands.

"Put these in the inside pocket of your coat. Keep them safe."

We each nodded as we accepted our packets.

As the grown-up moved on, Brid whispered, "And what if something happens to us?"

I shrugged and did my best to squeeze the papers inside my coat.

The Examiner was talking, her voice loud. All the children turned, at attention, to listen.

"We're heading north to the next train stop; with so many of us, we'll have to go on foot, but we should be there by morning. A train will meet us. We'll continue up to the sea, where we'll board boats to take us across to Eilean."

We were each handed a personalized yellow card. We all stared at them.

Leave Sofarende?

"These are your passes for the boats, in case something causes us to be split up. Get to the water and show this pass to any boatman, and he should take you across. Keep your military ID and clearance on you for entry into Eilean, but if Sofarende falls and you are taken by soldiers of Tyssia, it would be better to appear as child refugees, so destroy everything at the time that seems imminent: tickets, military ID, documents.

"If that happens, you were never here.

"This place did not exist.

"Let's go; keep up."

With that, we turned to follow her out through the back gate, forming a moving column.

When the Examiner paused, eighty shuffling feet behind her also paused while she spoke to a figure by the fire.

"Tommy."

He turned.

"You're coming with us."

"No," he said.

"Yes, Tommy, come on."

"No. I work downstairs now. I'm staying with them."

"There is no more downstairs. No one's staying. They'll all be dispersing for different missions. You're coming with us."

He shook his head.

"We've promised your parents we would do our best to keep you safe."

"Who cares? What's the difference now? I'm not a kid anymore."

"This isn't about you being a kid. This is about us needing your brilliant mind when we get to Eilean. Your colleagues' work will be in vain if we don't get there to receive it. You're coming. It's an order."

The young man with Tommy nodded to him, but Tommy still hesitated.

"*I'll* need you there, Tommy."

Tommy stepped over to her, and accepted his yellow ticket.

I stood still as the group continued to move on, my own yellow ticket in my hands.

Where was Annevi?

Miss Ibsen had said it would be impossible to lose Annevi.

What about Gunnar? Where was he?

"Come on!" Megs called to me. People hurried to keep up with the Examiner, who was setting an alarmingly fast pace at the front.

My heartbeat thudded in my ears.

*It is easy to protect yourself and your loved ones; it is harder to protect and care about others. . . .*

*Because other people matter, too . . .*

*Every person matters. . . .*

"Wait!" I yelled.

Megs, Brid, and Caelyn stopped.

"I have to take care of something," I said.

"No, you don't!" Megs said.

"It's part of my assignment."

Megs shook her head.

"Go, I'll catch up. Stay with the group. I'll call you here"—I pointed to her breastbone—"and catch up. It will be only a few minutes."

191

Caelyn moved first; she grabbed Megs's hand and ran, pulling her along. Megs looked back at me.

Once again, my *I love you* for her stuck in my throat.

She already knew, though. Didn't she?

I would be with her in just a few minutes.

I turned to run the other way.

I went into the garden shed, found what I needed there, and hurried back into the house.

Proctors still filled the main room, dragging evidence of our work outside. I carefully peeked down the hallway; all clear. I turned left to a back staircase.

Climbed the stairs.

Ran down another hallway.

And unlocked a door.

# 33

RAINER STOOD, PACING.

"What is going on?" he asked. "It is noisy. There is fire." The orange light glowing through the window was bright enough that we could see each other. "Is the building burning down?"

*Would* they burn down the building, too?

Maybe.

Would they let him out first?

"We're leaving."

He nodded.

"What—what happens to you now?" I asked.

"I should ask you that—what happens to me?"

"I don't know."

Rainer looked at my face. "Why have you come to see me?"

"I hope—no matter what happens—when you think of Sofarenders, you think of me."

"I will, Mathilde. But I do not want you to remember me and the things I said to you. The things I've done."

"I will remember this." I pointed to the blue painting. "That's how I'll remember you."

He nodded. "Take it with you."

I folded it, and put it into my coat with the other papers.

"I hope you get back what's in that painting, one day."

"Not me," he said. "But you, you might have your own beautiful blue world. You will build it yourself."

A lump rose in my throat.

"Thank you, Mathilde."

"For what?"

"For saying goodbye."

I was running out of time; I needed to catch up.

If it was treason to talk about Sofarende falling, then what I was considering certainly was.

But what would happen to Rainer? Would they let him starve? Shoot him? Or would it be even worse if he was handed back to his own people? His capture was dishonorable. He didn't have a home anymore.

Rainer had no weapons, but he could find some. He could hurt us. Or he could collect information and send it home. He could complete his mission in Sofarende.

But how upset he was about the school ... that meant something, didn't it?

I pulled my hand from my coat's outer pocket, and held up the clippers I'd stolen from the garden shed.

Rainer stared at me.

"Promise me ..."

He nodded.

"Promise me you won't hurt anyone. Not me. Not my family. Not my country. Nobody."

"I promise, Mathilde."

But this was war. Lying was a big part of it.

I thought again of what Mother had told me about protecting people. She would understand why I had to do this.

I didn't think Rainer wanted to hurt anyone, ever again.

I would have to trust him.

This was the world I was building. Where people didn't think only of the people they loved, but of the others, too.

I bent and clipped a big square out of the wires. I pulled the fencing away, and crawled through the gap far enough to hand the clippers over to Rainer.

Our hands touched, for the first time, and I met his eyes.

"Don't forget. You promised."

"My word, Mathilde."

"I have to go," I said. "Be careful. There are people everywhere."

I unlocked the door and dropped the key.

I paused, remembering.

I had one more stop to make.

The hallway of bedrooms was deserted.

In my room, I took down the handprints painting, folded it, and put it in my inner coat pocket with all the other papers.

My stomach clenched. I was going even farther away from my sisters, and they might soon be in trouble. I couldn't even tell them.

*They're counting on you to get through this. That's their hope. That's what all of this has been for.*

I made my way to the northern gate and ran through when no one was looking; I couldn't ask for help. The proctors would ask what I had been doing, and when they found out about Rainer . . .

*Please, please, please let that have been the right thing to do.*

I was a traitor to my country now. I couldn't pretend I wasn't.

*Catch up. Catch up and look like you've never been separated.*


As I pressed on through the darkness, I strained my ears for the group. They must have been told to keep quiet. The sounds of eighty feet should have given them away, but I didn't even hear that. I was afraid to call out after them.

So I reached for Megs.

*Megs?*

*. . . Megs?*

I let out a breath.

I paused, closed my eyes. Felt for her instead.

*My dearest friend, walking beside me.*

*Through the streets in Lykkelig, whole as they used to be. Then bombed and broken.*

*Through the woods we loved.*

*Through these woods now.*

*My dearest friend, with long dark braids.*

*Long dark braids, chopped short.*

I caught my breath as my eyes opened.

Megs would know I went to Rainer.

Would she guess what I'd done? Would she see it the way I did?

I stopped calling her.

Or maybe she wasn't listening for me.

I kept walking, but my legs ached.

The familiar rumble started up in the sky, and quickly became a roar.

I jumped against a thick tree trunk, peering through the leaves for the lights, the colors on the wings.

Tiger stripes.

But then, zooming from the other direction, came our own aerials, shooting at Tyssia's, lighting the sky with streaks of white, bursts of red. Explosions. My hands covered my ears.

Aerials fell out of the sky.

Would anyone survive those crashes? Would we have more Tyssian prisoners like Rainer? Or would *we* be the prisoners?

I kept going.

In the dark, flames and smoke rose ahead of me. My group wouldn't set such a fire. I waited as the flames lessened and the smoke grew, though minutes were passing. Maybe it was the enemy out there. But maybe it was Sofarenders who needed my help. Or who could help me.

When all was still, I crept forward.

It was a downed aerial.

The smell was atrocious. Like things that never should have been burnt. I covered my nose with my coat sleeve.

"Hello?" I called.

Nothing stirred.

I crept closer.

The great aerial, at once bigger and smaller than I had expected, was a mangled shell. Even its markings were burnt off.

This was Rainer's nightmare. My nightmare.

It didn't matter if it was us or them.

We were all the same.

We were all the enemy; we were all the victims.

We were all dead.

I stumbled away.

*You have to get to Eilean. Get to the train by morning. Or you may be a prisoner yourself.*

*A prisoner, or on trial for treason.*

*It doesn't matter if Sofarende wins; you're dead either way.*

*You have to get to Eilean.*

I repeated the directions, kept moving, but my brain was slipping, my feet unsteady.

I found a patch of soft moss beneath a tree, and curled up.

# 34

SUNLIGHT WOKE ME.

How could the sun be shining? Hadn't the world entered endless night?

When I'd fallen asleep, I'd still been in Sofarende. What had happened while I slept? Was this land still ours? Still Sofarende?

Perhaps it wasn't the sunlight that had woken me after all. Something was tickling my stomach. I raised my head to see a little squirrel trying to get into my pockets.

He reminded me of the woods back home.

I shooed him off.

I reached into my pocket and found two biscuits. We must have gotten them for snack during playtime one day. Had I really been so well fed at Faetre that I had forgotten two biscuits?

"Thanks for finding these, little one." I broke off a little piece and tossed it to him.

"Shouldn't you be afraid of people?" I asked.

Things couldn't be too bad if the squirrels hadn't run away.

"Have you seen any other children? A big group?"

"*Tich-tich-tich,*" said the squirrel as he ate the biscuit piece, spinning it round in his hands like a tiny wheel.

That probably meant no.

I sighed and got up.

I had to pee, and I was really thirsty. Amazing, really, how those problems seemed a lot more important than the fact that my country was being invaded and I was lost in the woods.

I did what I needed to behind a tree, half expecting this moment to be when the others finally appeared. It would have been worth the embarrassment.

I checked the sun's position, and started walking north. I didn't pass a stream. But there were some younger trees, tall and bendy; I shook them and opened my mouth to collect the dew. Not much, but better than nothing.

I took out a biscuit and munched as I walked along.

Had someone brought food and water for the children?

Would the Examiner notice I was gone?

Probably.

Ask my friends if they'd seen me?

Probably.

What would they tell her?

I swallowed hard.

The Examiner had wanted me to talk to Rainer. She gave me room to make choices. Would she have thought this was the right choice, or the wrong one?

The biscuits settled uneasily in my stomach.

Even if she had wanted me to go talk to him, she probably wouldn't have authorized me to let him out.

She would surely find out about it; she'd told Tommy the adults from Faetre were going to be in touch.

She had said she trusted me.

I needed to catch up, but what would happen when I did?

Soon the mountains sloped down to a field, and I ran across. Up ahead . . . train tracks!

I looked up and down the tracks. No station in sight. No people. No vibrations. Nothing coming.

The day had warmed. I took off my heavy coat and hung it over my arm, careful not to let any of the papers fall out. The sky was pure blue, the grass bright green.

No hints of war.

Except for me.

After an hour or so of following the tracks, I spotted the station, though it was a few more minutes before I reached it.

A country station, with its sign painted over.

Not that I cared one lick what its name was.

The paint looked shiny—still wet?

I pressed my fingertips to it; they came away black.

Panting, so thirsty, I climbed the steps to the platform and went to the ticket window.

"Excuse me?"

An old man peered through the glass.

"What a day."

"Excuse me?"

"You didn't care to get dressed?"

I looked down at my nightgown.

"Did a group of children come through here?"

"Did they? Did they ever. At five this morning. All in their nightclothes, too. Asked me if I had a radio. And a telephone. Then they told me to paint over all my signs. *All my signs?* I asked. And then some woman with them shows me her military ID, high up, ordered me to do as the children asked. Some of them slept on the platform, and then an unscheduled train arrived, with more people on it with those fancy IDs, so I didn't get any answers. All the children climbed on board, and that was the last I saw of them."

"So I missed them?"

"I'll say."

He sounded very grumpy.

"And they didn't tell you their destination?"

"No."

I bit my lip.

"I'd like a ticket on the next train that will take me to the Cairdul Sea, please."

"And why wouldn't you? Lovely day for a holiday. In a nightgown. Two orins for the ticket."

"Just a moment." I patted my pockets, pretending to look for a wallet or little purse. Should I show my military ID and order him to let me board? Start crying and ask him to let me catch up with my friends?

But then, in my inner pocket with all the papers, my fingers touched something smaller . . . an envelope.

I had totally forgotten.

I held the envelope to my nose, closed my eyes, and breathed in deeply.

Post office.

*Thank you, Father, for thinking ahead. How did you know?*

I sorted through the fat stack of bills, and easily paid the fare.

The man raised his eyebrows. But it certainly wasn't his business why I was traveling in my nightgown and carrying so much money.

My next question stuck in my throat; I'd had access to classified information, so I didn't know what it was safe to ask.

"So ... do you have a radio? Have you been listening to it?"

*Has Sofarende fallen yet?*

"Lots of bombings being reported. Like other mornings."

"Have you seen any Tyssia aerials?"

"Up here?"

I let out a breath.

"When is that train? And when will it get me there?"

"Assuming there's no more surprises with the schedule, eleven-fifteen. You should be there by five tonight."

There was no assuming. Not anymore.

Unless one assumed the worst.

"Could I have some water?"

He raised his eyebrows again, but disappeared from the window and returned with a small glass of water. I drank it in a few grateful gulps.

He took the minute to study me more closely.

"You're one of those children? Your nightgown is so dirty it looks like you climbed over a mountain. Where are you all from?"

"A school. Up in the mountains. Our school burned down in the night. They were taking us to shelter somewhere else. I was tired and lay down to sleep and got left behind."

He looked skeptical. I would have told him not to tell anyone else about us, but that would have been more suspicious. Instead, I tried to look pathetic and hungry, which I was. Hungry, anyway. But he didn't seem sympathetic, so I took my ticket and went to sit on the platform bench.

When the train arrived, I boarded. My ticket was collected, but the conductor eyed my nightgown suspiciously.

"Is everything all right?" he asked.

*Is everything all right?*

*Is anything all right?*

"Yes, sir. There was a fire in our house. We lost everything, so this was all I had to wear. I'm being sent to my grandmother's up north. My parents gave me some money to eat in the dining car; could you tell me where it is?"

He looked mildly surprised, but said, "Toward the front."

I carried my coat, listening to the crinkling of the papers. I didn't dare take them out to look at them.

I found a table and looked at the menu, wanting to order everything.

*Don't spend all your money.*

Who knew when I would be in the care of the Examiner again?

If ever.

*Don't think about that.*

As I watched out the window and considered what to choose for lunch, that particular trainy feeling came over me.

That sense of being neither here nor there, of being alone but in a great moving-forward kind of way.

I ordered meat and eggs. The waiter watched as I wolfed down my food.

"Chew a little," he said. "Don't choke."


The train pulled in to its final stop that afternoon—a busy port town. I walked along the sea, on a boardwalk; there was no sand. Ships were being loaded up or unloaded. People bought fried fish at stalls. Soldiers patrolled.

My breath caught, but I let it out.

They were our soldiers. Not Tyssia's.

Could I just show a soldier my yellow card and maybe he would help me?

The Examiner had said anyone would have to take us across.

My group must have left already. Or maybe they'd gone to a different town.

Men yelled at me and laughed about my nightgown. Kinder people asked if I was sick. I knew I was pretty dirty; I'd been able to wash my face and hands in the washroom on the train, but my tangled, loose hair was looking even more unruly in the misty air.

Looking out at the sea, I realized just what a great lot of water it was.

No Eilean in sight.

I put my coat on to keep out the damp and to cover my nightgown as best I could.

I would talk to the soldiers. That would be the best thing to do.

I found two by the piers. I took out my ID, military clearance card, and yellow transport card.

"Do you need help?" one of the soldiers asked. "Are you lost?"

I shook my head and handed him my cards. "I'm supposed to go to Eilean."

He read through my papers. He looked shocked.

"You haven't seen the others, then—other kids like me?"

He shook his head.

"I'm—I'm supposed to go to Eilean."

"And we're supposed to stay here," the other soldier said. "You're a lucky one. You can't imagine what that yellow card is worth."

His friend gave him a look as he handed the card back to me. "You hang on to that. Come with me."

He led me down the boardwalk to another pier and a fisherman younger than Father.

"You've heard all boats must volunteer to carry out military requests?"

Another nonvolunteering. The look on the man's face said he thought so, too.

"What is it, then?"

"Our young friend here must be taken to Eilean, immediately. Soon there may be a flood of people trying to go, but there's orders to get Mathilde out right away. Will you take her?"

He looked me over. I was starting to shiver in the sea breeze that tickled my bare legs, but I looked steadily back at him.

"What about fuel?" he asked the soldier.

"We'll get you filled up to head out. And a supply to return."

He nodded. "Course I'll take her. Not that I have much choice anyway."

"No," the soldier chuckled. "But this task isn't so bad."

"They bombing ships?"

"Haven't gotten their aerials far enough yet."

The fisherman nodded and extended his hand toward his boat.

Just a small wooden fishing boat. But it had an engine.

I had never been across the sea on a boat.

I had never left Sofarende.

"Thank you," the soldier said. I stared out at the dark water while he made the fuel arrangements. "Good luck," he said to me when they'd finished. "I hope your mission in Eilean goes well."

I had a mission in Eilean? I'd thought my mission was just to *get* to Eilean. But of course they wanted us to go there for a reason. Wasn't that what the Examiner had said to Tommy? That we'd expect to receive messages there?

"You had any dinner?" the fisherman asked me.

I shook my head.

"You'll want some. Food in your belly helps with motion sickness, weighs down the nausea. And who knows when we'll have the opportunity to get more. Go to the fish shack down the way—not the first one, they lean on the scales and overcharge—but the second one, that one's best—have a bite, and come back. I'll be here."

Would he be there? Was he trying to get out of taking me?

He smiled. "Go on, now. Don't worry. I don't mind taking

you. I have my own children; I'd be glad for the right person to help them if they needed it."

I hurried down the pier to the second fish shop. I bought a fried piece of fish wrapped in newspaper that became instantly greasy. I carried the fish back, biting into it as soon as it stopped steaming. Flaky and fresh, heavily breaded . . . it was so good! Maybe the most delicious thing I'd ever eaten.

It certainly competed with raspberry-glazed buns.

My heart thudded: this was my last meal in Sofarende.

Maybe ever.

I hurried back up the pier, licking my fingers.

He was still there. "Good grub, isn't it?"

"Very good."

He hopped into his boat, and offered me a hand.

I tried to get used to the wobbly feel of the boat as we passed the last of Sofarende's islands.

No Eilean in sight.

The sun set, and darkness surrounded us. When I looked back, I could no longer see Sofarende.

My home.

My home. Where I had let loose an enemy.

And become a traitor.

I checked in my coat: the papers were still there. The blue world. My sisters' handprints. I placed my hand over my pocket, feeling warmer, and a bit less wobbly, to know their small images pressed against my heart.

I carried a lot of things from home. Home including Faetre. All of Sofarende.

Not just in my pocket, but deep within me.

What had Megs picked to bring with her when she came to Faetre? I hadn't even asked. I'd been so surprised by her arrival—a gift from home herself.

She had brought news of our families.

Hope that we could be reunited with people we loved.

Those things were more important than anything else she could have brought.

And those were exactly the kinds of things the Examiner had wanted me to learn about Rainer. His memories, small pieces of his life that were important to him. And why they meant something to him.

He'd brought anger, yes.

But other things, too.

Things that we'd all brought.

The *idea* of home.

Safety.

Family.

Wanting to have the whole world set right, back to how things used to be.

If not the whole world, then our own small pieces of it.

I looked back over my shoulder, toward Sofarende, even though I couldn't see it.

A lump rose in my throat.

Father, Mother, Kammi, and Tye—were they all right?

Would someone tell them that we'd left?

Mother and Father would believe that we'd gone ahead somewhere safe.

It was what they had wanted. We had chosen that hope together, back in Lykkelig.

I turned my eyes ahead, looking into the dark for Eilean.

I remained standing, holding them all in my heart. Father, Mother, Kammi, and Tye; Megs; Brid, Caelyn, and Annevi; Tommy, Hamlin, and Gunnar.

Even Rainer and his blue world.

I would carry those people and things with me to Eilean.

And whatever happened when I got there, I would use them to build the world that I wanted.

One in which we could all be at home.

MATHILDE'S STORY
CONTINUES IN
THREADS OF BLUE

# ACKNOWLEDGMENTS

Thank you to the following organizations who provided access to the primary source materials, classes, and immersive environments that helped me imagine life, work, and family separation during wartime:

Dover Castle

Imperial War Museums, London, with special thanks to the Research Room

London Walks

Bletchley Park

Washington and Lee University

George C. Marshall Museum

The Intrepid Sea, Air & Space Museum

The New York Public Library

The Brooklyn Museum

# ABOUT THE AUTHOR

Suzanne LaFleur is the author of *Love, Aubrey; Eight Keys;* and *Listening for Lucca*. She lives in New York City, where she decorates her walls with the handprints of children she loves. Visit her online at suzannelafleur.com.